"Clipped Wings, They do FLY"

Clipped Wings They do FLY

By: William Michael Barbee

Authors contact info is as follow:

William Michael Barbee
Website: www.clippedwingstheydofly.com

Email: barrichinc@aol.com

Printed in the United States of America

First Printing: Jan 2012

ISBN 10- 0615579892

ISBN-13: 978-0615579894

TABLE OF CONTENTS

FOREWORD

It's an honor to be able to provide introductory thoughts to the novel "Clipped Wings They Do Fly" written by William Michael Barbee. When Mike first told me about his decision to finally write this story, I think I may have been more excited about it than he was. So when I found out it was completed, I couldn't wait to read it!

Once I started reading, one of the things I noticed was that some of the chapters began with a poem from the Author, which really adds a bonus to the reading allowing the reader to be drawn in emotionally before each setting in the story. In knowing Mike and the historical events he's seen in life and his family's contributions to "The Movement," I knew the details in the story would offer an unheard view to familiar parts of history. The years of notes, memoirs and poetry collected to form this novel is what really brings you in to the tale of Billy Ray Michaels.

The story details the life of Billy showing how he grows from an adventurous youth to him ending up in court for a murder he doesn't even remember committing. The character's relationship with women especially the dealings with his Psychiatrist and his Mother really allows the reader to understand the emotions built up within Billy's heart and his connection with his pets illustrates his bond and longing for family.

This truly is an amazing and recommended read; this unique psychologically teasing tale will leave you in suspense while you wait for the turn of each page.

~David L. Powell III

PREFACE

While in search of words to fill the gaps
That my emotions can't seem to find,
I'm left speechless in a place,
Confused in a world,
With my troubled mind!

It was the Oprah Winfrey Show that I fondly remember, this middle aged man, with droopy jaws and a scraggily beard, holding court to a tear-filled audience. I sat in amazement to hear all of what he had to say. His name is John Bradshaw. He's been labeled as *"The Psychological Guru for the New Age and America's Growth Expert."* He is a Clinical Psychologist who challenged these adults to look at the *"Child Within"* themselves. He told them that no matter how old they were, there's still a child within them who's been hurt, and neglected. He challenged me on that rainy day to look back to my childhood and embrace, grieve, and move on with the pain of the child who was abused, wronged, abandoned, and at some point may have been loved. He said that would be the beginning of my healing and understanding of how I can move beyond the issues I'm confronting today. In part, this became the beginning of my *"Infancy Exercise"* as taught by John Bradshaw.

It was his philosophy that I would later embrace through some of the teachings of my appointed Forensic Psychotherapist, Dr. Shelly Neiderbach. After years of depression and battling my own demons, I was blessed to meet this angel in the form of Shelly Neiderbach, who would later save my life. Through her intervention and guidance, I was able to hate without feeling the guilt of being honest with my feelings. She was the first person who told me that it was okay to be angry and afraid, cry, and even hate. She followed up by saying, *"Hate is just another feeling and it is unfair to deny yourself the honesty of your emotions, without being free to express them."* She also cautioned me not to live in that space! She reassured me that it was okay to finally free those caged birds that were locked within my spirit. She helped me regain confidence in my ability to fly on my own and to see through my *Invisible Wounds*. She reminded me that I can fly even in the roughest winds of criticism from those who never took flight with their dreams. It was then that my pen afforded me that freedom to fly.

Twenty-six years later, I was compelled to call Dr. Neiderbach because a friend was traveling through some of the darkest tunnels in his life and couldn't see any light. Just as I began to open my mouth in counsel to him, I could clearly hear her familiar voice speaking to me. After all of these years of not talking, this became the first and only time that I called this angel to thank her for redirecting me to my path of freedom. In doing so, I realized that my vulnerabilities would be exposed to my friend, but more importantly, I would be bringing to an end this long open chapter. For 20 long minutes of a tear filled exchange, in the company of my friend, I finally closed my book.

To bring this story full circle, in 2009, who would have thought that I would hire an individual who was struggling through some of the same issues in which I battle, only for me to reach back and bring closure to this open chapter. In addition, on October 28, 2011 my spiritual mother and friend to Dr. Neiderbach, Dr. Helen Hoch, of whom I haven't seen or spoken with, presented me with a large glass photo of me and her taken during that dark time in my life. It was so mind boggling and overwhelming that I began to cry.

Upon receiving this photo from Dr. Helen Hoch, she informed me that within 2 months of me placing that initial call to my friend, Dr. Shelly Neiderbach took her last flight.

However fictional this book may appear, it is derived from many of my real life experiences. Therefore, it is only fitting that I dedicate it to the life of my mother, Josephine Priscilla Barbee, Dr. Helen Hoch, and the memory of my friend and confidante, Dr. Shelly Neiderbach, the *"Sheros"* who saved my life.

Example

"Quote me not a scripture
Cause in the book there are many,
But leave me with your example
The same way you found me."

William Michael Barbee

Chapter 1
Passing Judgment

Maybe

I wasn't born bad.

I played football in a vacant lot.

I jumped rope on litter filled sidewalks.

*I leaped in a game of hop-scotch on broken glass-
filled pavements.*

*I played basketball on a rim nailed to my neighbor's
tree.*

I ran track with my brother's worn out sneakers.

And as I recall,

I was put back in school because

I spelled equality, beginning it with IN instead of E.

So today I sit confined to time,

Just wondering what went wrong

Cause

I wasn't born bad.

Poetry amongst other things has always been an escape for me. Whenever something goes wrong in my life, or when I'm extremely nervous about something, I escape by closing my eyes and fall into my security. That was a skill I acquired as a young boy, learning what some may say is the wrong way of handling problems and situations. No one ever told me that later on in life that my way of escape came with many consequences.

I was diagnosed with over five sleeping and mental disorders, but I think it's only three. I can never tell. All I know is that this familiar banging and voice yelling, "Defendant" is causing me to lose my train of thought.

As I begin to my open eyes, my only thought is to find where the thunderous banging which has interrupted my peace was coming from. My heart is

3

beginning to race as I look around and can only see uncertainty. A strange older white man sits right beside me and he's sweating so bad it's seeping through his suit. An attractive woman seems to be typing on a really small typewriter and along with everyone else she's ignoring the guy drawing the picture. Continuing to observe my surroundings I can't help but notice the armed guard standing beside two rows of empty wooden chairs. "Who is he guarding?" I thought to myself. Still trying to pinpoint the source, I noticed that this lady wearing a black dress, with a face that would scare a ghost, banging a wooden hammer and screaming gibberish. The only words I can make out are "sleep," screaming," and "contempt." "To whom is she speaking to?" I can only wonder. I just hope it's not me."

With the worries that it could have been me who was causing this Lady's outrage, I decided to fold my hands and remain perfectly still. While glancing at my wrists, to my surprise they're imprisoned by cuffs. It was then that I realized that there was blood smeared on the edge of the French cuffs. It wasn't long before I realized that I was wearing one of my favorite church suits. It too was stained in red. I began to take notice of my surroundings, since the room has fallen completely silent. I want to go back to my happy place within my own thoughts, so I smile as I drift.....

No sooner than I closed my eyes, I see twelve strangers entering the room behind the guard with the gun. Suddenly my surroundings are beginning to make sense and I realize that this is not a place that I want to be. I too began to sweat. My mind began telling me that "I needed to escape. I have to get out of here," my mind battles with the choice to run out in a blaze of glory or simply accept my fate. What is my fate?

"Will the defendant please rise," stated the judge. I just sat there looking around for clarity or some sense of awareness. I could only wonder at this point. The man in the suit sitting next to me stood and nudged me on my shoulder, motioning for me to stand. I quickly adjusted my tie, shuffled my jacket and stood next to him. I was nervous without a cause so I just shut my eyes as hard as I could, as I listen to the angry lady say, 'Mr. Casser this is my last warning about your client's disruptive behavior in my courtroom.' With shut eyes and sweaty palms, my knees began buckling slowly towards my chair. I felt as if I was about to stroke subconsciously as the pressure of my mind began allowing me to float off into my own subconscious.

On this occasion, there was no peace in my heart, only fear and hate. So it was no surprise that my psyche would take to a place that resembled those emotions.

I find myself lost in a recurring dream that I used to have as a small child. Where, what can only be described as a fire breathing mythological "Griffin" a half bird, half lion type monster is attacking everyone in my neighborhood and all I can do is watch. Covered in a blanket of terror, I cringe in thought that everyone else in the town was dead and the creature knew I was the only one left. I could see him searching me out, looking under the porch, down the ally, and around the corner. Now he appears through my window in the distance as our eyes meet from over 500 feet away. At this point, I only have two options; Flight or Fight. Either I could run my ass off and hope that I could succeed where others had fallen victim or I could stay, fight and conquer this beastly bird.

I chose to stay and fight. I figured if I tried to run and it catches up to me; I would be out of breath and won't have the energy to put up a battle. Why not just battle from the start? It was my father who used to say, "It's time to man up." As my heart and thoughts raced, the beast launched at me like a heat seeking missile. I scramble to find something I could use for my defense. The only thing I could find around me in this dark room was my sheet-covered mattress, so I quickly grab the top cover. I begin to roll it into a twist, as my older brother would right before he'd whip me with his towel during horseplay as he stood atop my bed and waiting for the beast to bust in to get me.

CRASH! *It slams through the window destroying the wall in an instance. I stood firm upon my mattress never taking my eyes off its eyes. Like an eagle it dipped its head low and proceeded to swoop in on me from underneath. Prepared, I whipped the cover in its mouth and bounced on the bed as hard as I could. Landing on the neck of the beast, I quickly turn around, grabbed the other end of the sheet and began to take control. Bucking like a raging bull the winged* creature showed his displeasure in being conquered by a mere child, by using calming tones and phrases I heard in old cowboy movies, "Easy Girl" "Woo now" "There, there" I was able to ease its discomforts and it seems as if it was starting not to mind me being up here. So I slowly moved the sheet from out of his mouth, and allow it to drape under its neck. Tranquil, the now gentle beast heads out the entrance it created and we take flight to the roof of the building.

Ostensibly linked as one, we noticed a survivor on the roof. We breathe fire on this lone human being which caused the house to catch ablaze. We began to move in closer to see if the human has survived and we noticed that it's my father. Full of rage he rushes at us with a shot gun in his hand screaming how much he hated us. He shoots his mighty gun and I feel this burning pain in my right arm. As my eyes closed, I feel a strong wind pushing against my face. We open our eyes to see that the ground was getting closer and closer. I fought to pull up; using the sheet but my arm is so numb I *can't lift any longer. As I look over at this beast's wing, it appears as if we have shared the same fate. Approaching closer to what will surely be a devastating splat; I see the wing fighting to regain its strength. It pulls up, avoiding the crash landing, but I still couldn't move my arm. I reflected, "Why, why can't my arm move, I thought we were connected? Did I not have enough strength to fight my father's attack?" Now I fall alone, forced to face life's gravel on my own, I guess I'll just shut my eyes because it's always safe in my sanctuary.*

Awaken by the echo of voices, I try to sit up, but my face and body feels as though I was beat with a bag of bricks. I assemble myself enough to rise. "Where the hell am I?" I said to myself, as I looked around to observe my surroundings. Lying below me was a hard mildew smelling mattress, which was much too small to be considered a twin. A disgusting toilet neighbored a crud filled sink near the wall of bars from the ceiling to the floor. I began to stand in order to get a better stance to listen to the voices dancing around the halls. I began to feel pressure in my throat and lungs; so much so, that I began to violently cough. Feeling fluid upon my hands and lips, I look down to discover blood. "What's happening to me? What's happening to me" was all I could begin to think. Blood flowing down my face and dripping through my sleeves, I began to panic. "Heeelllpppp, Heeelllpppp" was my cry. For the life of me I couldn't figure out how I ended up here and why the hell was I bleeding!

There was no answer. In spite of the voices that I heard in the hallway, it seemed the louder I yelled, the more alone I felt. I walked over to the bars and clinched them tightly as I screamed, "Hey, Somebody, let me outta here! Let me out of here!" Within minutes of my yell, I could see two shadows appear. I can now understand their conversation much clearer.

Male Voice, "records say that he wasn't, Doctor."

Female Voice, "Then that may have been the problem. I clearly explained to you and your staff my patient's sleeping disorders. This never should have happened.

Male Voice, "You're absolutely right mame, it never should have happened! He's right this way Doctor."

As they approached the bars, a certain familiarity in one of the voices lulled me into bashfulness. I haven't felt this way in a long time. This was the same feeling that I had when I was a child. "Am I being shy or nervous?" I questioned. Sometimes my ability to separate what is from what's not is divided by a very thin line.

Female Voice, "Bill-ly, Bill-ly." It had to have been the most beautiful sound, the

way my name rolled off her tongue
"Bill-ly."

I look up and said with excitement in
my voice, "Dr. Neiderbach, Dr. Shelly
Neiderbach, Is that you? Oh my
goodness! What are you doing here?"
Dr. Neiderbach was standing next to an
armed guard. She was wearing a blue
business suit with a "V cut" white
blouse. "I love me some Dr.
Neiderbach," began to roll off my
tongue. She was the first white woman
who I ever met who sported an afro. I
first met her some years back when I
was going through some stressful
situations. Somehow, my primary
doctor medically appointed her to me
because they used to say I had sleeping
disorders. I overheard them telling my
mom that I needed to be placed on
Ritalin to calm me down. I grew up not
understanding if I had a sleeping
disorder then why should I be placed on
that type of drug. It wasn't til I met Dr.
Neiderbach that I was actually told that

I was Schizophrenic. In spite of that early diagnosis, I always respected and trusted her for always being honest with me.

She always wore the sweetest perfume. Whenever near, it always spoke to me. It was as if I'm running through a lavender garden sprinkled with accents of Japanese Blossoms. "Am I in love" or "am I lost in this wilderness of confusion". She's so beautiful in my eyes. However awed I was by her presence, it still couldn't explain how nor why I'm here. She finally answered, "Yes, William! I'm sorry that I forgot you like to be called Billy for short. Well, it's me. I was called here because you had another trigger and they needed me to come give an analysis to make sure everything's ok. How are you doing? Are you okay? For the life of me, I couldn't answer any of her questions. I was still speechless as she continued, "Do you know where you are?" I looked around and responded with uncertainty, "Dr. Neiderbach, I'm scared. I'm scared. I don't know where I am." She first gave a nod of uncertainty. She then responded saying, "You're in Essex County Court House, and you were held in contempt for falling asleep during your trial, standing on the prosecutors' desk and causing a disturbance in the courtroom?" I beamed with a look of confusion as I thought I just closed my eyes for a second, so I explained, "Contempt of court? Trial? There is no way! Why would I......? Trial? I don't even know what I'm doing in court in the first place. The only thing I recall is waking up in the nasty room with blood on my face and arms. I want to know who, why, what and when? I was attacked but I don't know who did it. Are you here to save me?"

She looks to the guard and said, "This is worse than I thought. Can you leave us alone for a minute; I really need to talk to my patient?" The guard nods his head and exits the same way he came in. Once he leaves, she breaks out a tape recorder from her purse. She then asks me if it's okay to record the conversation. I then gave her a nod of approval. She proceeds to place the recorder up to her sultry lips and says, "Billy, I am going to be recording this interview for my records. Patient's black outs are appearing more frequently with elevated stages of memory loss. Patient, Billy Michaels appears with small lacerations around the forehead and blood on his sleeve. To answer your questions, you were not attacked, while you were irate on the prosecutor's table, you reportedly took a nosedive onto the floor, inflicting your own wounds. As for the duration of your stay, you will only be in this cell throughout the weekend and you will be transferred first thing Monday morning."

I examined my wounds to see if there is any validity to her explanation. As far as I'm concerned, there's still no way I can know for certain. At this point, all I can do is see what I have to do to get out of this dilemma. So I said, "Ok, Dr. Neiderbach, say I did cause a scene in the court room, what is it I could have possibly done to end up imprisoned in the first place." She was slow to respond, "Billy, I'm not at liberty to divulge or discuss your case with you. I'm here to help facilitate your recovery so that you can stand on trial to hear your fate. Billy, I've been your psychiatrist for over 20 years, so I'm not totally surprised about your condition. What surprises me is your inability to accept the situations after you revive from your blackouts. You should have passed this stage with the medication I prescribed. I want you to start back with the method of regression and we're going to start by going back to your earliest memory."

Chapter 2
Clipped Wings

Hymnal

Looking back on this life of mine,
I was taught that a man isn't a real man
If he desired to sing or dance.

It was embedded into my head that
Grace was a quality given to women,
not men
Because, "real men played the dirty sports"
So I grew confused in being
Who I am

I opted to paint,
To express the blues and hues
Given to me by my brush.
I chose to run
And eat the breeze
That dance could afford me with.

Whether or not, lied or denied.
Then, the opportunity to sing or dance.
In my heart, a hymn always hum
To the time of my last dance.

So now openly as a young man,
I sing and dance
To the beats of
Of my own hymns.

"Bill-ly, Bill-ly!" I hear the sweetest voice calling my name, causing me to open the eyes that I don't even remember closing. "Billy, where were you just now," asks Dr. Neiderbach. "O, I'm so sorry Doc, not sure what happen there, was I asleep? "Yes, somewhat. You seem to close your eyes and shift the subject of your thoughts into somewhat of a tangent, after attempting to answer my question. "The last thing I remember was that you were asking me about my earliest memories and a poem I wrote when I was young popped into my head," says Billy. As I looked towards her, I notice she began to write something on a note pad, during this time she doesn't even look up to acknowledge me. "Did I do something wrong Doc," I asked. That was my concern. I didn't know if I was going to be accused of doing something wrong again while I was asleep. She takes her sweet time to bring her attention back to me, as she utters, "No, nothing wrong. I just needed to take notes for my records. Don't worry, it's nothing bad. She then says, "So, I see you have been using your poetry as I suggested since you were a teen to regress your memory. What memory does that poem take

20

you back to?"

Billy says, "Yes ma'am, a lot of what you taught me over the years, I've been able to utilize on a day to day basis. You said that whenever I felt anxious to just take a few moments and breathe. So that's exactly what I've been doing. Now to answer your question, when I think about that poem, my earliest memory takes me to the time when my family and I first moved into our new home. I was just turning six years old and heading to first grade. Our family consisted of the seven of us; my four older siblings, my parents and I. It was a two-bedroom apartment in the West Ward of the City of Newark. Most folks who lived in our neighborhoods didn't own their homes. Yes that's right; we were one of many apartment dwellers in this poverty-stricken neighborhood where 7 tenants comfortably lived together in a 2-bedroom apartment. Often, the den or family rooms became bedrooms while the dining room became the living room, and the living room became the 4th bedroom.

As far as the streets are concerned, crime was a thing of normalcy. It was as if we were jaded by its plight. It was like the Wild, Wild, West, fighting, stabbings and shootings all around us. It seemed as if our neighbors became accustomed to just doing things any old way. To some degree, I think we would forget what was right from what was wrong. Down the road was this brewery with the nastiest smelling odor that one could ever muster. The vacant lots adjacent to our home and my friends' homes became the baseball, football, rock throwing fields that many of your most gifted kids honed in on their craft. I was known for being very athletic. I ran fast and threw a football further than the next guy. I wasn't too bad for a street-baller. Well, I use the term street freely. I knew the limits of the streets so the baller part only reflects my abilities as an athlete. The streets were dangerous. However, *during that time in my life, there was so much that I wanted to do but I felt I couldn't because of my own fears of not being accepted.*

I can remember pulling up squeezed together in the back of my father's Oldsmobile Custom Cruiser station wagon. One of my dad's favorite George Benson songs, "The Greatest Love Of All," was playing on the 8-track cassette player. I fought back the urge to sing along as the car jumps the curb knocking me back into my sister Jeannawillis, who was reading a book.

I knew all the words to that song, but my inability to conquer my own demons had taken control of my tongue. I was what they called shy. Jeanna, while ever determined to achieve the best for herself, was the middle child and always focused on her studies. As far as I recall, she has never gotten a grade lower than an A her whole life on any exam she ever taken. I don't even think she noticed that I bumped her as her eyes are still glued to the book.

'We're home,' Daddy screamed, "We're home," as we approached this green three story house with the top floor windows boarded up and the remaining windows all had bars on them. "Kids, this is your new home, Daddy said. I was somewhat excited when we first pulled up to this old house because it was sooooo big. Did I mention that we lived on the third floor? In spite of Daddy's strong demeanor, he had a funny way of expressing it. He made us feel as if the third floor apartment that we were moving to could have very well been considered the Penthouse. I couldn't help but notice all the trash that filled the front curb atop our door step and the abandoned car, which had no doors, tires, seats or engine parts, covered with graffiti. There were guys standing on the porch, but seem to move only when daddy got out of the car. I saw kids playing in the streets, with no regards to traffic. "Hey, git out. We're Home" yelled my father.

My oldest sister Martha, jumps out the car first full of glee, 'yes! I'm finally gonna get my own room.' Even though she was my sister, she played more the role of a second mother to me. She was overly protective, making sure I got everything I wanted. I guess all I needed to do was cry and watch her take from my brothers all of their belongings just to sooth my wants. Maybe that's what caused the wedge of envy that my brothers project towards me now. Anyway, Daddy began yelling once again, "Git out!" While rushing out of the car, we fell over one another like items on a conveyer belt. Here I go, last and least of all, just falling out over Antney's foot onto his new Pro-Ked's sneakers. Luckily my twin brother Albert helped me up. We weren't identical twins, or for that matter twins at all, but we were the closest in the house. We did everything together. We shared clothes, shoes, dreams and even whippings. I truly can say that back then, he was the best friend that life could offer. Whenever anything happened to me, he always had my back.

Albert and I sprinted to the front stairs once he helped me up. When we arrived, I looked back and there's my father standing next to our oldest brother Antney, who was as cool as the spring breeze, holding a box of his belongings. I quickly tap Albert to get his attention and the look on his face causes my sisters to stop and look back too. Daddy yelled at us to get back over to the car. We all proceeded to walk back with our tails between our legs preparing for the verbal thrashing that we knew was sure to come from our militant father. For some reason that George Benson song was still playing in my head, so I began to hum the tune. As soon as I opened my mouth to spew the lyrics 'I believe the children are the future......,' **Slap!** My Daddy back hands me across my face and said, 'Give me that noise, singing like you a celebrity.

In the midst of my story, Dr. Neiderbach interrupted me asking, "Did you say that your father struck you?" I quickly responded saying yes. She then proceeded to ask, "What made him do that?" I could only answer saying, "I don't know, that's just how Daddy was. It was like he had a switch that turned on and off. Hey, it's just the way things were then." With a look of

surprise she said, "Okay, you can continue.
I think you were saying something about
your singing."

I began, "He said you ain't no celebrity, and
you better not start crying like a little girl,
because you're neither. What is wrong with
you jokers? Did you forget we have a car
full of stuff that I bought for you and your
momma. I swear you monkeys don't
appreciate nothing. Get your sorry behinds
over there and start unloading that crap.
None of ya'll got a key anyway. Jeanna and
Martha, help your mother. Antney, Albert,
and Billy git ova there and git that mess out
of my Custom Cruiser. Ya nappy headed
bread burners don't know how to act
whenever you're in public.'

With our happy smiles glued upon our faces,
we proceeded to unload the car helping each
other carry bags and boxes into the house.
Sometimes it seemed as if he treasured that
car more than us. One of Daddy's pet
peeves was that he didn't like to see
frowning faces. His favorite line was, "Do
you want me to give you something to frown
about?" My Dad is one of those kinds of
people that you have to accept the good with
the bad. I think his experience in the Korean
War really took a toll on him. I truly believe

that he only wanted the best for us. I think he just had a hard time conveying the sentiments of his compassion. Though he yelled and often laid his hands on us, he was still a great provider, sacrificing a lot for us and always making sure we were taken care of. One of the interesting things that always comes to mind is how daddy would constantly remind us of every sacrifice he made for us, good or bad. Even though, we still loved him.

Daddy began leading us into our new home. We marched and marched, to what seem to be an endless path. From the first floor to the second floor, we marched. We were like a duck that leads her flock. Finally, we can't go anymore. Daddy was all the way up front, while mommy, Martha, Antney, and Jeanna followed. Albert and I weren't too far behind. Daddy appeared somewhat excited to be leading us to a better life. They said that we were only moving here for a short while, just to save up enough money to buy a house in a better neighborhood. I couldn't for the life of me understand why we had to move, leaving all of my friends Ricky, Keithie, Jay, Kenny, Mookie, Maurice, Wayne and Ira behind. Mommy tried to be reassuring by telling me that I will understand it when I got older. It seemed as if that was the excuse for whenever my parents couldn't answer a question posed by my siblings or I.

At last, the final step! Daddy tries to open the door for the first time with much excitement written all over his face. I guess he felt he needed to psyche us up hoping that we wouldn't be disappointed in the home he chose for us to live. He stuck the first key in the door but to no avail. He then put the second one in and struggled with the key until the lock gave in to pressure. I immediately took notice to the fact that we weren't the only tenants that were going to be occupying this home. In addition to the apartment doors that we passed on the way up, there appeared to be two existing families already residing in our new space. They were the Greys and the Brown families seemed to follow us everywhere we went. We thought we left them at our last place of residence. We used to live in a different part of the city. That house became infested with mice droppings and roach eggs when the state built this highway (Interstate 78). In hindsight, I think that was the origin to Albert's respiratory complications, smelling all of those roach eggs and mouse droppings. Nonetheless, we just continued to move in, ignoring them in the process.

Everyone was taking their rooms, all but me and my twin Albert; we were really looking forward to sharing a bigger room. My Momma calls for Albert only. This is strange because she always called us as if we were one name like, 'Albert William'. Regardless, I went along too because I didn't want to be left alone. 'Yes'm,' I replied to my mother as if it was us she called. 'I called Albert, William gon' head back downstairs and finish helping your father boy, I need to talk to ya brother.' I turned around with tears in my eyes and slowly left the room. I knew I had to suck it up because I wasn't allowed to show any type of sensitive emotions, especially if I were to be present in front of Daddy. No way could I let him see me crying like a fag again, no way. At that point I was like a faucet. I shut off all of my emotions and started down the stairs.

'Hey Billy, come back here for a minute,' Momma called out to me. I quickly ran back to her with a huge smile on my face. I was sooo relieved that she kept me from going all the way downstairs to meet my father by myself. On the way to her I ran through my new living and dining rooms. I don't know if it was bigger than our old one or if I was just lulled into a state of fascination with my new surroundings. Finally I arrived to find out what Momma wanted me to do. Boy, you just don't know, I love my Momma. For some reason, she was looking as beautiful as ever, holding a box with my belongings in it. She tells me in her thick southern accent, 'Come herr with me boy, we'r going to ya new room.' "What new room Momma," was all I could say. We passed what I thought to be Martha's room. I don't know if she assigned the rest of them rooms, but at that point it didn't matter. We were headed to my room. I got a little nervous because I didn't want to be in a room by myself. My only thought was whether or not Albert was going to join me. Continuing down the hall, my nerves are on edge, not only because I'm being separated from Albert, but because the darkness combined with the shrieking of the wood as we stepped, sent chills down my spine. 'This is it,' Momma says as we approached the very last room at the end of the hallway. It seemed as if it was the darkest room that I had ever been in.

As soon as Momma cut on the lights, all I saw was the scattering of the roaches as they ran for cover. 'Ya room's is right herr, you becoming a big boy now it's time you had

your own," she said.   My own what was all
I could wonder? Before long I realize, I had
my own bed, the bottom of mine and Albert
bunks. I looked around and noticed that
there ain't but one window in this room.
This has got to be the smallest room I had
ever seen. "This a closet," I said to Momma.
She smiled and said, "No son, this ain't no
closet, this ya room!"   I then repeated what
I had already told her about the room being
a closet. Momma then grabbed my hand
and said, "son, look in this mirror." Without
uttering a word, she gave me a look that told
me no matter what I thought of this space, it
was my room and if I questioned her again, I
might get the daylights slapped out of me.
She then said, 'My room is on the other side
of this wall and I wanted you close to me.
And since you're the baby of the house, I
wanted you to be in a room with the fire
escape, in the event we had an emergency.'

'What fire escape momma,' I asked. She
grabbed me by the hand and took me to the
window and opened the blinds and revealed
a metal platform that led up to the roof and
down to the second floor. This amazed me; I
never knew such a thing could exist. She
showed me this fence that unlocks, and
drops down to make a ladder; but she
quickly raises it back up. I start to look

around and ask, 'Momma why do we need a ladder that goes to the roof?' 'Oh' the family that used to stay herr were fanciers to those flying rats and kept a pigeon coop on the roof.' I had never heard of a flying rat before, immediately I thought of some type of crossbred creature with four legs, a tail and wings so I said, 'wow momma flying rats on the roof, you gotta let me see.' As I headed for the ladder, she stops me in my tracks. 'No boy, not flying rats, PIGEONS, folk just call em flying rats, don't be silly.' This explanation didn't cure my disease of curiosity as we exited the platform; I knew at the next opportunity I had, I would go back and check it out for myself."

Billy, Billy, was all I heard as me and momma was talking about the fire as it fades away. "Bill-lllyyy, are you okay? I'm beginning to have some concerns," Dr. Neiderbach said while interrupting my story. "What's wrong Doc? What concerns you?" I asked. She replies, "We have held many sessions over the years and I never heard you mention anything about the Grey and Brown families. Who were they?" I started to chuckle a little to myself, "sorry about that, growing up in the hood I just assumed everybody had them in their homes. "Who are you referring to William? The Grey mice and Brown roaches." Dr. Neiderbach smiles and says, "Oh okay, sorry to interrupt please continue your story."

For a second there I almost forgot I was telling a story, not realizing how long I was talking, she appeared to be part of my story. "As I was saying Dr. Neiderbach, we were settling down in our new home everyone was happy about their new rooms and even though I was separated from Albert, I have to say that I kind of like my own bed as well. In spite of the congestion, having that small window in the room gave me a sense of freedom. I knew that I could look out of it and dream about flying high above, like a bird. It was the very next day that I recall so vividly. It was a day that I was told something I never expected to hear.

Dr. Neiderbach interrupts again asking, "What happen on that next day?" Oh well, it was the first time that I had ever been separated from Albie. "Separated," said Dr. Neiderbach. "Yes, separated. All of our lives up until that point, we did everything together. We were practically identical twins. When he went right, I went right. When he went left, so did I. She then said, "So what happen on that next day?"

"Well, that morning my Mom called everybody for breakfast. She had a habit of waking me up first. I think that's because she still regarded me as her baby. I would help her in the kitchen even though I believed my Daddy hated seeing me there. He didn't know how often I would help mommy because he left for work at 5a.m. every morning for his first job until he was finally laid off. In hindsight, he may have thought that I was too soft for being his son and that his boys don't belong in the kitchen. Nonetheless, I was still a "Momma's Boy." Prior to that, the early mornings became me and my Momma's time together. Normally, everyone would rush to the kitchen table dressed for school. What was most surprising about this sight is that my twin, Albert was also dressed at the table. We're both usually dressed in our matching pajamas during breakfast. I had no idea why he thought he was going off to school, and besides, without me. I look at my Momma with confusion over my face and asked, 'Why is Albie ready for school? Ain't we is too young for school?' My siblings were all snickering to themselves as if there was an inside joke and I was the only one on the outside. My Momma looked at me and said, 'Albert's starting first grade today...' I interrupted her and said, "I better get changed too." I could only wonder why no one told me to ready myself for first grade. As I headed to leave the kitchen, Billy,' my Momma called out, 'You ain't fiddin to go to no school boy, Albert's a year and six days older than you boy.'

I look towards my brother to see if he would deny it and to the contrary, say something. He had the biggest smile on his face, almost as if he was happy to be leaving me behind. "Billy, don't cry, but I'm bigger than you." Hearing that didn't mean a thing. I just ran from the kitchen until I tripped over the saddle in the door and began pounding my hands on the floor. Even though Daddy was home, this was one time that I cried aloud, in spite the fear of him hearing me, I cried. I got up and began running again, back to my room I ran. Nothing would be able to calm me down from the deceit and betrayal I was feeling.

Many thoughts were running through my head, what else have they lied to me about, who am I going to spend the day with now and how come they wouldn't have just told me the truth. Now in my room surrounded by the shadowy darkness of loneliness and the sounds of the Greys running through the ways, I just sat on my bed and stared at the crying boy in the window. **Shriek!** The sound echoes throughout the hallway revealing someone was approaching, I could feel eyes beaming a hole in the back of my head and I turn around expecting to see my brother Albert but to another surprise it was my Momma standing in the door way. She sat beside me and said, 'Don't worry baby, you'll be going to school with your brothers and sisters next year.' I then looked up at her, eyes flooded with unshed tears and said, 'yea but me and Albie never been apart, who's gonna play wit me while everyone's at school?' She wipes the tears off my face and says, 'get dressed; I'm fiddin to take you to the playground.' It was as if a bomb of excitement went off. My face lit up with excitement. I loved to run away in the playground. Running was like breathing, the faster I ran the better I was able to breathe. I quickly got dressed and met her at the front door. Because this was our first full day in the neighborhood, I was curious to see what the new playground looked like.

I recall us arriving at the playground. There was trash and debris all over the place. If truth be told, it wasn't til I got older that I realized that the same playground that we used to play in was no more than a vacant lot. Most of the lots in the neighborhood were taken over by the neighboring tenants whose homes were next to them. Often they would plant vegetables and flowers and create beautiful gardens. In hindsight, it was those lots and playgrounds that became the hallmarks of my life. The playground that momma took me to didn't have a garden. It was a mixture of cemented stones from the basement of the previous building. Most significantly, there was this old man wearing tattered clothes throwing bread at these birds that gathered around him. That was my first time seeing such a sight. 'What are those birds there Momma?' I asked. She replied, 'those are the flying rats, boy, the pigeons I was telling you about before.' 'So, those are the Pigeons huh?' I asked. She just nodded in agreement as I continued to explore the playground.

There were lots of kids there my age but I was always shy, it was my brother Albert who was charismatic or as Daddy would say, a people's person and able to make friends quickly. Me, I always keep to myself until someone approached me and even then, I didn't always respond. It was as if I was afraid of being around strangers. I always thought that they wanted to do something to me. I vividly remembered when I was about 3-years old when Albert and I attended this Afro-Centric School called 'The Chad'. One day while sitting on the stoop waiting for momma to pick us up, this man in a car parked curbside called us over. I just ran in the building screaming at Albert to run, but to no avail. Albert just moseyed on down the steps to where that man was in his car and had a conversation. So maybe that's why I wasn't too social when it came to playing in the playground. I look at everyone who I didn't know as a complete stranger. It wasn't til I saw swings that I began to play. They were about 20 feet away from the milk crate where momma was sitting. I dashed over the trash and broken glass, heading straight to the swings; diving head first through the chains, landing on the seat stomach first, 'Weeee!' I yelled out as if I was flying, as I swung back and forth posing like superman. "Be careful Billy, be careful," echoed from my mother's soft voice.

We had to have spent about two hours at the playground before my Momma decided it was time to go back home. Normally, Momma would clean up the kitchen and her bedroom before my Daddy returned from his first job.

Dr. Neiderbach interrupted asking, "I

thought your dad was at work?" I quickly responded, "Oh, I thought I told you that he was laid off. Well, in any case, he was home." "Okay, continue!"

"Well, we went home. Momma and I were both exhausted, so I asked, 'Can I take a nap momma, I'm tired.' She smiled and nodded saying, 'go head boy, I'm fiddin to take me a nap too.' When I realized she was going to sleep on the couch in the living room because daddy was still asleep in their bedroom, I knew this would be the perfect opportunity to check out the roof and see exactly what was up there. I dragged myself into my bedroom, carefully glancing over my shoulder to see if momma really was about to fall asleep. It wasn't long before momma was fast asleep. I then proceeded to open the window very slowly, not wanting to make any type of extra noise as to alert my Momma of my going ons. I see the ladder to my right and looked at it as if it was Mt Everest I was about to climb. I put my right arm on first, I remembered that vividly, then I shot up there like a canon loaded with excitement. I was in awe from what I saw. It was an opened wooden framed cage with fencing as its body. I slowly approached the cage as it was covered with close to a dozen birds. My

39

thought was to get close to the door where I would then be able to contain them and turn them into my pets. To no avail, once I reached the coop the Pigeons all flew off in a panic.

There was a smaller one that fell to the ground and began flopping around. This terrified me to no end but I couldn't look away; I just stood and watched to see what was happening to the bird as it struggled to get upright. Only one of its wings were flapping at this point. It was barely lifting off the ground and kept falling on it's side. Finally it mustered enough energy to stand. It appeared to be looking in my direction as if it knew I had been watching it this whole time. I slowly began walking over to it to see if I could pick it up and put it in the coop. The closer I got to it, the further it moved away. So I started towards it. I figured it wasn't going to come willingly to me. 'Yes!' I screamed out as I finally caught up to it. I slowly lifted my head from my prize and noticed a huge shadow over me, 'What in the world are you doing up herr boy?' The sound of the roaring voice causes me to jump and in the process I dropped the pigeon. 'Yes Daddy,' I replied. He says, 'Turn around and look me when I'm talking to you boy. Ya Momma said you were taking a nap; I came to check on ya and hear all this ruckus. I asked you a question, what you doing up herr? ' I turn to look my father in his eyes, though it was hard for me to do, I just blurted everything out as fast as I could because I was so nervous. "Nut'n," was my only response. Often when put in a tight situation, our first response to any question was, "nut'n". It took me a second to think. I knew I needed to think and think rather fast. So I said, 'Momma showed me the fire escape so I went on it to see how it worked. And when I got on it, I heard some noise so I followed the sound and saw the pigeons on the roof. And when I got up herr, to see them, they all flew away except for this one that fell down and now he don't fly no more. Then you got herr Daddy, that's all Daddy.' He looks at me and looks at the bird and says, 'Ya Momma should not have shown you of all people that fire escape.

It was then for the first time that I saw another side to Daddy. He said we can't tell anyone especially ya Momma bout this. She hates birds. I didn't know momma hated birds. Well on the other hand, maybe because I was young that I didn't pick up on her description of them, as flying rats. "Now let me see it," My Daddy grabs the

41

bird with no hesitation from me. 'Just as I thought, the lil guy clipped it's wing,' he says. 'What's clipped it's wing mean Daddy?' I asked. He replies, 'It means it has a broken wing, hold on to him boy, I'll be right back.' I did just as my Daddy told me I held the bird and didn't move one inch. He returned a few minutes later with a first aid kit. 'What's that for Daddy?' I asked. While grabbing the bird from my hands he begins walking to the coop while saying, 'I'm gonna wrap a bandage around it's wing so it's bone can heal but even with that, the bird may not fly again. That's a tactic I learned in Korea." Daddy served in the Korean War and related everything he did to some type of military experience. If you want him to live then he's gonna have to be your responsibility.' When he said those words to me, I felt something I can't explain. It was like he was treating me as if he loved me. This was something I was going to take seriously as I tell my Daddy, 'I will take good care of him Daddy. Don't you worry.' After he bandaged the pigeon he put it in the coop and showed me how to open and close it, we slowly left the roof together."

Huff, Huff, I coughed, forcing me to interrupt my story. As I looked up, I see Dr. Neiderbach looking up from her note pad with an expression that told me she wasn't ready for me to stop the story there. She proceed on saying, "O, that's very interesting, I would like to hear a little bit more about your father but, if at all means possible, let's talk more about your youth. Is that Okay?" I could only respond yes because I would love to talk more about me growing up in the jungle.

Chapter 3
My Jungle

"Doc, did I ever share that poem with you about my jungle?" Before she responded, she took a deep breath, as if she had to prepare herself for another one of my long stories. I really didn't care. I just wanted her to hear more about my childhood. She looked at me and said, "I can't truly say that I remember that one." I responded by saying, "I wrote that some years ago when I was, hmmmm....I don't know; somewhere around the age when I first met you. You asked me to write a story about my relationships with my family and friends. I remember the first thing that came to my mind was *My Jungle*." Dr. Neiderbach just smiled as if she was enjoying what I was saying and then asked me to recite it. "Let me write it down so that I will remember it." Okay!

My Jungle

I see you in my mornings
Chasing after you pay,

Why don't you stop and redirect my
brothers
Who minds have gone astray.

They're Lost in a land
Full of hypocrisy and confusion,
While they smoke and sell your drugs
To create a form of illusions.

Many of us are lost and blinded
By the smoke of oppression,
So please help us to rise
Out of this grave of depression.

Some say our problems
Exist solely in our minds,
While others say the slums
Are where these problems, you'll find.

You pass laws that tax
What little we earn,
But you live in the outskirts, the suburbs
And don't even know my concerns.

By now it's afternoon
And you'll run back to you stay,

A soft pillow in a crib
A mansion is where your head will lay

Election time and passing parades
Are the only times that we seem to
meet,
With problems of education, drugs, and
crime
Why won't you come to our streets.

We live off of Springfield Ave, Spruce
Prince St., and Pennington Ct.
These are places that you seem
To never come.

So, tomorrow in your travels
Please stop to ask
What is this Jungle about
Before you pass!

I always seem to be running for my life.
In my neighborhood most of my friends
called me "The Bird," because of my
ability to soar in most street sports. I
was always the fastest. None of my
brothers or sisters could ever keep up

with me, no way; 'I was too fast for them'. Some would say that I didn't run, but that I took flight. I ran so fast that many compared me to the Sankofa Bird because as with the bird, I always looked back at those I left behind. Ha ha ha, I remember the time when Albie and I were at the local grocery store when three bigger boys came up to us to rob us. I said, "Albie run, run Albie." Before I realized, I just ran and ran til I reached the porch steps only to find Albie nowhere around. I went back around the corner to see where Albie was. He was still talking to those guys. I yelled, "the cops are coming." Those guys ran one way, while Albie ran straight to where I was standing. We raced back from the grocery neck to neck. In spite of the robbery attempt just to get Mommy the food for breakfast. I'll never forget that by the time we got home, all dem egg was broken. Daddy sure wore our hides out dat day boy I tell ya!

"Billy wake up, **CLAP!**" Dr. Neiderbach said as she yelled out while clapping her hands to get my attention. "You were talking as if you were a child with a southern accent, it seems as if your mind keeps transcending to that of, when you were a child. And as far as I remember, you were born in Jersey. Do you recall what you were just talking about?" She asked.

I looked around to see what was around me and replied, "No ma'am, I can barely remember anything we've been talking about for the last two weeks." So I asked Dr. Neiderbach, "Do you have any idea of when they'll be letting me out of here?"

Blanketed with confusion she firmly said, "Billy, you've only been here for a few hours, not two weeks. I see your condition has gotten worse." "What condition?" I asked, but she seemed to have ignored the question. I sit waiting for her to respond but she just continued to take notes. Finally after what seemed like three hours of silence, she looked back up at me and said, "Maybe it was because you were just telling me about your childhood that you got lost in those recollections. You started off this regression with mentions of your siblings and your neighborhood. Let's go into that for a minute."

There weren't many things I wanted to remember from my childhood, thoughts I would forcibly push out. I know that keeping something away from Dr. Neiderbach would only cause trouble for me. So choosing my words carefully I proceeded to talk about my neighborhood and my siblings.

"A couple years after learning that I wasn't a twin; my brother Albert and I still remained the closest of my siblings. At the time, my best friends were Albie, my Momma, my cousin Chrisie, who was deaf and Flappie. Flappie was the name I gave my secret pet Pigeon that lived on our roof in the coop. It was the bird that my father showed me how to tend when he first caught me on the roof. I would sneak out many a night through that window and climb that ladder of serenity and feel free as a bird while I sat and would just stare off the rooftop; so being on that rooftop made me feel superior.

In my dreams, I always thought I had wings like a bird. I thought that I could fly, fly high. Maybe it was because of my hopes that one day Flappie would take to flight. I loved taking care of Flappie so much that I would risk a butt whipping if ever I got caught going to check on him. Therefore, I would always use stealth-like measures to assure that I wouldn't be caught again and made sure I was in bed before Momma made her rounds to check in on all of us in the middle of the night.

I would try to secure at minimum 6 hours of sleep because most mornings in our home always seemed to be the most hectic time when it came to using the bathroom. Often momma would wake one of us up before she went to work, but by the time that person was suppose to wake everyone else up, they'd fall back to sleep, making all of us late for school. I remember we would always have to shout out," I got first preference: or,"I got next." I still laugh when I think back to how my siblings would take advantage of me since I was the youngest and the smallest. One morning while we were running late for school, three of my siblings, Albert, Jeannawillis and Antney burst into the bathroom while I was sitting down on the toilet. Antney ran to the sink to wash his face. Jeannawillis jumped in the shower to bathe, while Albert stuck his toothbrush under the faucet of the sink while Antney's prepared to wash up at the sink. I sat there on the bowl trying to get them out the bathroom without losing my spot. This may seem strange to many, but it was normal in our household. Somehow and someway we made it through those times. It was those times that we seem to always remember the most.

Even though we were poor, we were raised to value all of our possessions. We didn't live in a modernized lavish apartment house. We lived in a building that had been built in the early nineteenth hundreds. Besides, lavished living wasn't seen in our neighborhood because most knew nothing about it. Most of our furniture was bought second hand. Momma wouldn't hesitate to go to the local Salvation Army or Goodwill Mission on University Avenue to purchase furniture or appliances for us. She taught us an early age the true value in second hand shopping. I wouldn't hesitate to say that she coined the phrase, "One's man's trash is another man's treasure." I often remember us bringing home the used furniture strapped to the roof of my father's Oldsmobile Custom Cruiser station wagon. To us, that used furniture was just as good as new money straight from the printing press.

I can also remember how momma would load us up in the station wagon and ride us all day on Saturday mornings to the suburbs of Livingston, Essex Fells, Bernardsville and Short hill, NJ to the garage and estate sales. She didn't have a care as to what people thought we looked like because the bottom figure was that money is green no matter where it's coming from. As I reflect on that time, those people must have thought we were coming up there to rob them or something. A car load of black folk in their neighborhood, what would one think? Contrary to popular belief, they were actually kind to us, with the exception of a few of them, watching our every move. Albie and I would sometimes play hide and seek with them even in their homes. We still laugh at the thought.

I would say that those trips truly helped me and my siblings to appreciate and value some of the 'finer things' in life because it was our first opportunity to see how people with money lived. Not only did we see how they lived, we talked, walked and bought the same possessions that they owned. In my imagination, Momma was consciously teaching us a lesson on life. A lesson that is ever present today in each of my siblings' lives. In spite of one's financial situation, my mother wanted us to dream beyond the poverty that we saw outside of our doorsteps.

Even though we were able to venture out into other neighborhoods, many of our neighbors were not as fortunate. I may need to rephrase that and say they chose not to leave their environment. Momma always told us that people tend to imprison themselves way before other think of shackles. Therefore, I always believed that, *"a person's world can only change around them only when they're willing to make a change within themselves."* This same belief was echoed though the ferocious voice of the Rev. Jessie Jackson in the 1984 Democratic Presidential Campaign when he said, "It's one thing to live in the slums, but it's another thing to have the slums live in you."

By not leaving our neighborhood, many of my friends parents formulated their own views of what looked good. It was quite obvious that our taste differed from theirs. I called them our 'ghetto fabulous' friends. This didn't make our taste any better than theirs, but it was just reinforced within me that taste is relative. In spite of that relation, I still maintain the same view of them as being plain old gaudy... If truth be told, I'm sure they would say the same about our taste, despite our concepts of what looked good. Many of them thought that lavished apartments meant that others thought they had money, but that wasn't so. The same could be said for

the drug dealers who lived next door
who owned the Mercedes, Porches, and
Jeep Cherokees but rented from a
slumlord.

Many of these same neighbors must
have thought that since no one in the
hood was any better off than the next
man, they had to be the first to project
success though either the cars they
drove, furniture they bought or even the
clothes they wore. It seemed that most
of their furniture was on some type of
lay-a-way plan from Valley Fair, Two
Guys, N. & S, The Credit Doctor or
either they were renting it with an
outrageous interest rate. I think most of
their concepts of what looked good
came right from that box called a
television. On TV, it was nothing to see
Liberachie with his golden trimmed
piano and silk drapes that fell from his
window panes or watch Hollywood's
perception of what was beautiful.

I remember when I first went to Gavin's

home. Gavin was my neighbor who lived across the street from us. His parents always seemed to have more than most of our other neighbors. Almost every two years Gavin's mother Mrs. Jackson bought herself a brand-new Cadillac while Mr. Jackson kept his same old Chevy Impala each year. I fondly remember the first time I went into their home. Man, if you could only see how their house looked on the inside, you'd laugh." They put truth to the phrase, "you can't judge a book by its cover." They had contact paper with zigzag designs that they thought were somehow related to an Andy Warhol painting series, glued to every appliance in the kitchen; they had plastic on all the dining and living room furniture as if they truly believed that it would one day be saved as a collector's item and many, many more weird mis-educated ghetto concepts. Maybe that is why I was never truly surprised by the degree in which they sought to uphold this status image among our neighbors of success.

Our parents raised us to value self worth and self esteem. It was embedded in our heads that it's not all that important what people think about you, it's what you think about yourself. That may sound nice to say but I still battled with issues of low self-esteem. It was truly a shame that most of our neighbors worked hard at proving to others that they were something when all the while they should have been proving it to themselves. Sometimes I still look back on that and chuckle because all of us were poor as hell. Besides, who then had something to prove?

There were other neighbors in our hood who didn't seek to prove anything to anyone. They seemed to be angrier with themselves. They would dress as if they didn't have a penny to their name. Their clothes would be dirty, hair uncombed and more often than not, they'd be cursing like sailors. Every time when you saw them, they would either be sitting on their porch playing hid Wisk, Spades, Tunk or trying their hands at a game of 500 from early afternoon to midnight. Also in the day, you could watch them making trios to the corner store to purchase cigarettes and lottery tickets. It seemed as if most of them never went to work or even looked as if they had jobs. I always marveled at how much money they would spend on things such as lottery tickets. One time I went with my friend Ricky to the corner store to get his mother's tickets and that woman had to have played at least $25 worth of tickets. For some unknown reason to her, she never won. It was funny how she'd pick all of her numbers from her psychic and zodiac books which were suppose to line up the winning numbers with some significant date in her life. If gambling was a religion, I guess she would be considered a priest.

In spite of these circumstances and conditions, as a community, most of our neighbors were relatively close considering our differences. Often I remembered Mrs. Codney knocking on our third floor window with the handle of her broomstick. It seemed to me that she would knock on our window about 6pm every evening. Sometimes she and my mom would talk for five minutes, while other times they would speak for at least two hours. Many neighbors communicated like my mother and her next door friend Mrs. Codney. It must have been too easy to just pick up the telephone and make a call or just walk next door and visit a friend.

It was always funny when my parents were watching their favorite television show, when all of a sudden you'd hear a disturbing banging at your dining room window. I can even remember sometimes Mrs. Codney would have her son Jack knock for her. Jack brought his own humor to the situation because he had a bad stammering; he just didn't take the time and talk slow enough to gather his thoughts before he spoke. Instead of asking for aluminum foil, Jack would make it one word like, 'Lum-Fal.' My dad loved being the one to respond to Jack's window call. He would try to get Jack to repeat his question at least five times. In retrospect I felt sorry for Jack because he couldn't help his stammering. 'Jack, now what you say? I didn't hear you! Try again! You need what? Son, what did you say you need?' In spite of that, Jack still remained strong with confidence asking for what his mother sent him to the window for. My father always had a way of taking things too far with some of my friends especially when we were playing or disturbing him while he slept. Through time and peace I found in my elevated solidarity, I was able to find ways to cope with…"

Interrupted by Dr. Neiderbach, "Billy, what are you trying to mask here? I can't put my finger on it, but it seems as if you're purposely avoiding specific details in your childhood. I can't fully assist you if you're not willing to be completely open with me. I'll try to rephrase my questions a little more to further help you get to the memories you're obviously withholding. She then said, "You briefly talked about a bird being one of your closest friends and how it bothered you seeing the bird with a broken wing. Can you tell me more about the feelings that you experienced whenever you felt the urge to go upstairs to the rooftop and tend to a bird with a broken wing?" I just looked at her with a solemn stare. I could only wonder why she would want to travel down this road. So, that's when I took my time and told her the story behind my broken wing.

"One day while Albie and I were playing. My mother's sister asked if we would like to go to the store for her. Albie ran, so I was left standing there to answer her question. I clearly was at a loss for words so I answered her honestly. I told her "no," because she asked me if I'd like to go. Momma always told me that I could tell the truth to anyone as long as I wasn't disrespectful. Well, my aunt just looked at me and walked away. By the time I started walking down the stairs to where Albie ran, I could hear a big boom, as if someone fell out of the bed. Before I could turn around to see where the noise was coming from, I felt the wrath of God, my father's hand grab me in the back of my collar. He was half dressed with a wife beater t-shirt and boxer drawers. He said, "what did you say boy?" I was completely confused as to what he was talking about. The last time I had any words with him was the night before when he said goodnight. So I was at a loss again.

As my aunt watched, with a smirk on her face that almost resembled enjoyment, my daddy beat me down and back up the stairs with his fist to my head, neck and side. All I could do is cry. I was always afraid of him because I could never predict his next move. I thought he was a crazy and angry man.

He never gave me an explanation as to why he was hitting me. That made me even angrier. I just wanted to escape. I went into the backyard to look for a close-pin from the laundry line so that I could make a makeshift splint. I found one on the ground so that's when I placed my finger between the two of the wooden sides and placed tape around to hold it in place. It wasn't til later when Albie approached me very timidly asking, "What are you doing?" I told him, daddy broke my finger for no reason. Albie looked at me surprised as to what I was saying, so he then asked me, did you tell our aunt 'no' about going to the store?" My only respond was 'yes.' It wasn't until then that I realized that he beat me for telling her the truth. Albie told me that I should have just said yes and went to the store. It took me years before I was able to comprehend what he was trying to tell me, even though I never agreed with my father's actions.

"Excuse me Billy, do you think that's why you dislike your father because he beat you for no reason," asked Dr. Neiderbach. I told her no, that wasn't enough of a reason to hate him. I hated him because he broke my finger! When Albie later told him that I created a splint from mommy's clothesline, he then called me and asked me 'what's that', while pointing to my finger. I said with the shakiest voice, "you broke my finger." It was then that I got another beating for accusing him of breaking my finger. Dr. Neiderbach looked at me with much concern and asked, "Did he ever ask you how you were feeling or where your pain might be?" "No, he never asked me anything. He just did his thing to me." I tried holding back my tears while telling her this story;

after all, it was over thirty years ago. I think that was the first time I saw Dr. Neiderbach tear from a story that I ever told her.

She reached in her bag for a Kleenex to wipe her tears. While wiping her tears away she still was able to talk saying, "Now Billy, I'm sorry for what you had to go through. That's truly a sad story. So is that why the broken winged bird meant so much to you?" "Yes! It's not just because of a broken wing, I just felt as if it would feel defenseless. Its wings were its only means of escape and without them it was doomed. I felt that I needed to step up for once in my life and speak for the weak because they like me, never had a voice. She then asked, "How old were you when this happened?" I quickly responded, "Somewhere around ten or eleven." She could only respond saying, "Wow! You do realize that those things that your father did to you weren't your fault?" I could only look at her as she appeared to need more time to gather her next line of questions. I felt bad that I told her the story because she seemed to form an opinion of my father that I had long resolved with him. I didn't want her to judge him for what he had done some thirty years earlier so I thought it was best to tell her about some of the good things that my daddy did.

Chapter 4
Daddy

I Still Stand

I once bore the burden of hate,
A fireman's hose, charging horses
Galloping over my bruised rights.
Crying out for freedom with tears of
Bloodshed, dripping down my body,
A red fall

German shepherds yelling out my name,
Chewing on my brothers and sisters
While they stood focused on there aim
It's no game; they lie for dead in a drain.

They jacked my mind,
And imprisoned my dad
To diminish his rights as a man.
Billy clubs dressed in blue suits
Disguising the law with injustices.

Despite the proclivity of man ability
To oppress/depress one rights of equality,
I still stand focused on my aim.
For my story shall speak whether or not
I lie dead in a drain.

Though I felt myself flashing through the thoughts of negativity about my Father; I can't help but admire him for the man he was and the struggles he had to overcome. Whenever I think about perseverance and strength, my father is the epitome. I proudly say, whenever I speak of my father, "Daddy was a great man," he use to tell us stories of his past in so much detail that I felt as if it was me living vicariously throughout his stories.

Through his storytelling, I began to develop a hatred for the white man. I hated what he had done to my Daddy and to people of color, by denying them of their civil rights. In most cases, blacks were denied the right to vote and freedom of speech. Daddy even said that in some cases, black were given tests in order to prove their ability to vote. These tests consisted of impossible questions, knowing that no one could pass them or give an accurate answer. Some of the questions asked were: *how many bubbles are there in a bar of soap or how high is high?*

My siblings and I grew up on the tail end of the Civil Rights Movement. However, daddy felt it was imperative that we remained conscious to the sacrifices that generations before us made for our freedom, human and civil rights. Even though my father told us these stories when we were young, it seemed as if I lived through every bit of pain, disgust and anguish that he had endured. We would sit and watch the television, it felt as if I was in a time machine. It allowed me to own, as if it were mine, every police dog bite, each Billy club hit that was ordered by the man in the blue suit, as well as, each derogatory word cast against my dad, my grand dad, my great granddad, my great, great granddad and so on. I even went as far back to own my ancestor's abductors and abusers, their whips and ships, their lies and denials to my ancestors' human rights. I just wanted to own every pain cast against my people. Owning these wrongs meant that I vowed never to forget who I am or how I got to where I am. In spite of all this acknowledging, I guess the most shocking realization came through learning that it was my own ancestors in Mother Africa, who sold my very ancestors into slavery.

"Billy, excuse me for interrupting your story, but was your dad directly involved in the civil rights marches and how did his involvement change or shape your life" asked Dr. Neiderbach.

"Well, yes he was involved in the civil rights movement. Back then he was a member of the local NAACP chapter in his hometown of Richmond, Va. He also followed closely the leadership of A. Phillip Randolph and became a committeeman with his job's local union. Daddy was one of the union officials who organized his regional local members to join in the struggle by participating in the "March on Washington. He was deeply involved and committed to the struggle."

After hearing about daddy's experiences and struggles with civil and human rights, I felt led to join my generation's movement. It was through my dad's involvement in politics and social issues that my interest was sparked to make a difference in the lives of my generation's people. In October of 1995, I was determined to make my presence count in Washington, DC at the Million Man March Rally. Even though I didn't agree with everything that was being said from the dais, I was more rewarded by knowing that my presence meant that in some way I began to own my dad's experiences and his presence at the 1963 March on Washington.

This movement was headed by the Islamic, (NOI) Nation of Islam Leader, the Minister Louis Farrakhan. To many of us in attendance at the march, the movement symbolically represented the 1963 March on Washington. Minister Farrakhan represented to some in attendance at the March a modern day Malcolm X, who in the early 60's made his call to justice. We gathered in the nation's capital to unify the role of the black man to his family, community, economics, the struggle, and most importantly to self. In spite of people's dislike for the Minister Farrakhan, the many Blacks, Whites, Spanish, Asians, and Indians who stood shoulder to shoulder in the Mall of the Capital in Washington, DC overwhelmed me.

I neither favored nor disliked Farrakhan. He's always had a lot of controversy about him regarding his involvement in the death of Malcolm X, the man who he once saw as his mentor. Minister Farrakhan reminded me of the differences between the Messenger and The Message, meaning you don't have to like the messenger even if the message is good.

In my eyes, Daddy symbolized what the whole civil rights movement was all about. When I stood alongside my brothers gathered in the Mall of the Capital, I couldn't help but think of my father standing in this exact spot. Though he never said it, I know he was proud of me, knowing that his legacy will be written daily through the lives that his kids are leading. I wanted to stand near the tree that he climbed while he listened to Dr. King deliver his moving speech, "I have a dream." I wanted to ride in the motorcade of thousands of buses, cars, and trucks racing up and down highways with my brothers who were hungry for knowledge. I wanted to see that Lincoln Memorial, and read the Gettysburg's Address. I wanted to look at the Capital, as it sat in the distance of those stories that daddy told. I wanted to hear the echoing effects of the megaphones as each and every speaker conveyed their thoughts. Daddy said that the power of the megaphones in my ears would make me believe that God was speaking directly to me. I needed to rub shoulders with my brothers from South Central LA, Chicago IL, Houston TX and even my homies here from Jersey and New York. I found myself embracing and crying with brothers from Louisiana, Kentucky, and Florida to mention a few. We just needed each other's embraces, whether we knew each other or not, we needed each other for that day in time. We were determined to pick up the mantle and return to our neighborhoods and families with new energy, love, and hope for our future.

"What did you do once you returned" asked Dr. Neiderbach. "Nothing" was all I could say. She was shocked by my response, so she asked, "What did your dad do once he returned home from the march?"

Upon my father's return from the 1963 March on Washington, he told us that he was more determined to make a difference in the minds of the black and white people locally. He said that he wanted the black man to become more unified in the struggle for equality. He wanted the white man to end the bigotry, hatred and fears he had for our people. He had a hope that this racism would end before my generation became adults.

Daddy began to seek leadership roles in his local NAACP Chapter. Through that organization, he became active with voter registration drives, equal opportunity networks and labor laws. Also within the organization, he reached the office of secretary and treasurer for the local chapter. In spite of the roaring cries and calls to unify that rang at the March on Washington, Daddy always said that his inspiration came from him watching the work of union organizers and (BSCP) Brotherhood of Sleeping Car

Porters Leader, A. Phillip Randolph. He was also moved by the strong degree of unity that he felt amongst the black brothers and sisters who were members of that group. He took that same practice of organizing people under a united front into the work force. He would later retire after a career of forty plus years working in local union as the only Black Committeeman on the Bargaining Committee.

He would proudly reflect on how the NAACP and other organizations would sponsor various artist and performers to entertain the protestors as they rallied on different campgrounds. Many people needed a catalyst to get them motivated. These rallies served as a means for gathering the support of the common people who ordinarily would not have outwardly supported the movement. Back then, Daddy was a limousine driver for Newark Airport Limousine Service. He said that Sammy Davis jr., Sidney Portier, Dick Gregory, etc. would entertain the demonstrators at the rallies; sometimes as late in the hour as 1am. He said that even Tony Bennett, the entertainer tackled the courage to support the civil rights rallies. After seeing their dedication to the movement, Daddy, was even more inspired to perform himself.

Daddy wasn't a renowned performer. His name was not written on the marquee at the Carnegie Hall, the Apollo, Cotton Club, neither was his voice ever recorded on the local radio, he was just another talented singer who never pursued his desires to perform professionally... During some of the smaller local rallies, Daddy would schmooze his way over to the podium so that he could steal the attention of the few who were assembled. There, he captivated their ears with his melodious voice. He was happy just being in the limelight. He had a strong and genuine love for singing. His trademark song became 'Oh Danny Boy.' Daddy said

that no matter where he went, they
always wanted to hear this short man
sing out of his soul, "Oh Danny Boy."

Daddy was a regular at many of the
local bars, clubs and nightspots around
town in spite of his strong church
upbringing. He just went from one spot
to the other establishing new contacts as
if one day he was going to mount out on
his own and become the next Nat King
Cole. He performed in some of Newark,
NJ's more prominent clubs. Some of
them were The Skate land on Branford
St., Prince Hall on Irvine Turner Blvd,
Key Club, etc.

In spite of the fun and joy that daddy
got from being in the lime light, he said
that emotionally he struggled between
his desire to sing and his conscious
efforts to speak for those without a
voice. He said that our rights still
remained his optimal concern. He, like
others, didn't perform only for the
pleasure of performing. He said they

performed out of their commitments to ease the burdens of their horrors of yesterday. He said that the entertainment was only a temporary resolve or high to their long-term struggles and that they still had to remain adamant on their focus of equality.

As it pertained to the Civil Rights Struggle, Daddy always spoke of A. Phillip Randolph, Dr. Martin Luther King Jr, and El-Hajj Malik Shabazz, better known as Malcolm X. He spoke of their common need for people of color, but also spoke of the difference in the approach that Malcolm X, Nation of Islam and the Black Panthers sought. He said that they practiced the old adage, an eye for an eye. To some, they believed that violence was the answer. Many just wanted a quick end to the government's acts of injustice against our people. However needed, it becomes unfortunate for some to truly understand that no quick solution can remedy a long-term problem, a problem that has existed for some four hundred plus years.

Daddy said that Brother Malcolm represented that leader who commanded respect, not only from the white man, but also from everyone he encountered. He began telling us about Malcolm's childhood and the horrific murder of his father. He also spoke of how a man with an extended criminal record, if determined, can rise up from that demented state and becomes an outspoken voice for many. I guess Daddy was trying to show us through Malcolm's experience that we should never give up on things, no matter how bad things might appear. He believed that Malcolm was that man; because he represented the anger and rage that he and many blacks felt during that time, but was not willing to outwardly express it. It almost seemed as if Daddy idolized Malcolm. He told us how Malcolm organized, through his religious organization, the Nation of Islam, blacks to do more for the community in which they live. He said through Malcolm's direct impact, black people began to own their own and build businesses within their communities. With all of what daddy said about Malcolm, it always bothered me that Daddy never owned his own home or business. I guess that is why I watch more of what people do rather than what they say.

"Does that still……..?"Dr. Neiderbach began to ask. I didn't respond to her because she just kept asking me all of these questions before I could ever finish my story. "So I continued…….."

I began to believe that Daddy and Malcolm both believed that the white man was the devil and they had no good in them. Besides, how could the black man trust he who enslaved him. Daddy said that Bro. Malcolm preached to the black man that he should not wait for the white man to give him anything, but instead, take control of himself and the community in which he lives.

I was born a couple of years after Malcolm's assassination. When Daddy told me that Malcolm was killed by blacks, it really bothered me. There was something about that phrase that stuck with me, "Chickens come home to roost..." maybe because I never really understood it until I was much older. I always thought about my birds in the pigeon coop on the rooftop of our three-story walkup home and wondered if one of them was hurt/different, would the others kill it. Just knowing that the accused assassins, who killed Malcolm X, came out of our hometown of Newark truly is disturbing. Daddy said he knew one of the 5 accused assassins who killed Malcolm. He said that Benjamin Thomas, Leon Davis, Wilber McKinley, Talmadge Hayer, and William Bradley were all from the same Masjid 25 in Newark on S. Orange Ave.

Daddy said that Minister Louis Farrakhan had just spoken at that Masjid before Malcolm's assassination.

I couldn't understand why black folks who were suppose to be fighting the same enemy would turn and kill each other. Daddy said that the NOI was not ready for the new Malcolm. He said that Malcolm publicly denounced the NOI leader, Elijah Muhammad as an adulterer. This new Malcolm no longer hated the white man. It wasn't until Malcolm went to the holy land of Mecca that he realized that the same white man of whom he was taught to hate was the same person who he prayed, laughed and worship with while on his pilgrimage. Furthermore, it wasn't that he embraced the black clergy's approach either, but instead, he had a renewing of his faith once he realized his American Islamic teaching limited him from the truth beyond the walls of their American temples. Through Malcolm's pilgrimage, his respect for Dr. King and others grew.

It was Dr. King and other clergy members who sought to instill the power of Gandhi's nonviolent methodology into the hearts and minds of the black people. It was the black clergy who stayed firm on their convictions that bloodshed would lead to more bloodshed; therefore, making any radical approach counterproductive. Had more people practiced in that belief of violence and bloodshed during that time, the progression that has been made today would have lingered for years to come. And besides, how could one defeat aggression without the necessary backing of their government.

I remember as if it was yesterday. Mr. Walter Cronkite, a CBS news Correspondent announced, 'The famed Civil Rights Leader, Dr. Martin Luther King jr. was assassinated outside of a Memphis Motel just moments ago.

Again, I repeat, the famed Civil Rights Leader, Dr. Martin Luther King Jr. was assassinated outside of a Memphis Motel just moments ago. Please stay tuned for further details.' In retrospect, I think that was the very first time that I ever saw my daddy cry. It was if he was the one directly wounded by the assassin's bullet.

At first, daddy froze from the disbelief of Mr. Cronkite's news. Then he screamed out at the top of his lungs, 'Why? Why? Why? Why did they have to do that to him? Why?' After hearing the noise from the other room Momma yelled, 'Danny, Danny, what's going on in there?' Startled by the noise, with alarm and curiosity written all over her face, Momma ran into the room while dragging me on her skirt to see what was going on. There she found my father kneeled on his knees, clinching his fists tight and pounding the floor. Momma quickly ran to his side, grabbing him tightly, asking him,

'What's wrong Danny, what's wrong?'
No sooner than she uttered the question,
she too began to scream at the
television, as if it had done something to
her. My siblings and I were so
frightened watching our mother and
father respond to the television with
such emotion.

After hearing the awful news, Momma
too collapsed to the floor into Daddy's
arms crying. Embraced one to the other,
they motioned us to their side. We
quickly ran to their aid, not even
knowing the totality of the events that
were just occurring. With tears in my
eyes, I quickly grabbed for my father,
while my other siblings embraced my
mother and one another. To tell you
why I all of people would embrace he
who I feared, I could not say. I think in
retrospect the support that I offered him
gave me a sense of power, since he now
appeared weak and overwhelmed with
emotions. I believed that he needed me,
and only me. It was only my support

that he would cherish because he could now see that I am strong enough to be his son.

While embraced, our parents continued rocking, holding and squeezing us tight. That became our posture for the remainder of the evening. As we rocked, momma began to moan and hum gospel songs one after another... I believed that she hummed all night long, from 'Amazing Grace' to 'Precious Lord' and 'Sweep over My Soul.' Kneeling into our parent's arms, still frightened from not the totality of the incident at hand, we began to cry. I guess the only thing we knew was that we needed the closeness that only our parents could give us. And again, we cried and cried and then cried some more.

Daddy wondered how anyone could use violence against a man who lived and stood for peace and non-violence. How could his fate be so contrary to live for peace and died in violence? He began to rock and cry out his love for us. Daddy began telling us how much he loved us. I think that was the very first time that I ever heard those words from his mouth. I didn't know if he was speaking directly to my brothers, my sisters, or me. I just knew he meant every word that he said and it was now my job to receive it from him, even if it didn't come in the way that I wanted.

For the remainder of that evening, daddy spoke of how he and others would march with Dr. King and other non-violent advocates up and down the stairs of many of our City Hall Building fighting for our right. Often, he said that they would get locked up and thrown in somebody's jail for the night until their bails were posted. I believe that it was then that my daddy said that Dr. King wrote his famous letter, from the Birmingham Jail. Along with Dr. King, my Daddy and others in cities across America expressed their views, angers and frustrations against a government that continued to fail in its promises of equality and justice. Daddy said that in some of these cities, the local police would allow their police dogs to attack the elderly, women and even children who marched. In other cases, the local mayor would order the firemen, along with police to hose down with force, the peaceful demonstrating marchers. Daddy also told us about the garbage man's strikes, the sit-ins at Woolworth and McCory's, voter registration drives and the bus boycott. It was then that I first heard about Rosa Parks and how she refused to give up her seat on a bus to a white man.

It seemed as if just listening to my dad's stories about the civil rights struggle left me in a state of rage and anger. Daddy always assured us that it's totally okay to be angry about something, especially when it's wrongfully cast against you. More importantly, he said how you release your anger when it's wrongfully cast against you would determine the outcome.

I believe that the strongest man is the one who could hold back his anger while walking steady in the midst of adversity. For to fight fire with fire would only kill the dream and without the dream, there would be no future." I guess you can say through respect, love grew for my father and I appreciate all he's done for our family.

I remember one day when my Daddy picked Albert and I up from the Chad School. That must have been the first time that I had ever seen my father angry about going home. He tried his best to tell us about what was going on in our community, but I'm sure we were too young to fully understand. It was as if he wanted us to be prepared for the worst, even if it meant his death. Daddy had a way of showing his passion for those things that he adamantly believed in. I still wonder how he could have thought we would have been relaxed after watching how nervous he was. This was the day that the National Guards were sent into our neighborhood to bring the control back to the local government after several nights of rioting and civil disobedience.

They were stationed at the corners of the streets in our community. These militiamen, most of whom were white, had their weapons within view for everyone to see. It made you think of a state of martial law. With straight faces, they stopped everyone who dared to return home to make entry into their city streets. If these soldiers goal was to intimidate the residents of our community, they accomplished it without question. I remembered as we approached our street, there wasn't anyone walking or driving. The streets were completely deserted. It seemed as if someone ended the party early, just before we arrived and forgot to let us know. The only ones that were present were these six National Guard members who sat on the bumper of their jeep cleaning their M-16 semi –automatic weapons. As we approached where they were stationed, one by one they approached to our vehicle. My father thought that he and these men had some kind of commonality amongst themselves, since they were at some time or another, the protectors for the United States Government.

"Bill-lllyyy, Bill-lllyyy," was the call that interrupted my thoughts. It was Dr. Neiderbach interrupting me to ask, "Why do you say that your dad thought that they had some kind of commonality between them?" I quickly responded as if she should have known, "My dad was a Marine. He fought in the Korean War." Her interruption was needed because every time I tell that story about those National Guards being at the corner of our block, I get mad. Daddy told us how things were back then and he later explained why the government brought the soldiers in our neighborhood.

"Anyway, as I was saying……" Of the six soldiers, two of them appeared somewhat agitated by our presence. Unfortunately for us, they would be the two of six who would linger around us the longest. I remember one of the soldiers motioned to the other soldiers, as if he and another one of his friends wanted to be alone with my Daddy. As the other soldiers returned to their jeep, the two remaining began what I call an assault of questioning as to my Daddy's whereabouts. It wasn't as if they really felt concerned to know where my dad was coming from. They just wanted, from what I saw, to intimidate him in front of us and belittle as a man. It was as if belittling him gave them a sense of power.

I could see that Daddy was getting upset with the process of what was going on, but there wasn't much he could do to change things. He tried very politely to answer all the questions that they asked him. I was afraid for those men because of the fact that I knew what Daddy could do to someone whenever he was upset. Believe me, I've seen with my own eyes what he can do because he did it to us. If these men stood a chance with my dad, they'd better leave him alone. He would occasionally look over at Albert and me. Albert was up to his normal routine of asking the second soldier about the tattoos on his arm. Albert told me that it was a red flag with an X in the middle of it. I asked Albert what it meant and he said it represented hate. I, on the other hand, became very upset and scared at what he had just told me. I didn't know what was going to happen to us. My only thought at that time was whether or not my Dad was going to try kill one of them because that's how he described the behavior of some of the Korean soldiers inflicting hardships on POW's during his war period. He said that the soldiers would dress in their normal attire, hiding a grenade and an automatic weapon under garments while pretending to be ordinary observers.

Well, the one soldier who was asking my Daddy questions began to get somewhat loud. He got up in Daddy's face, beaking the brim of his hat on Daddy's forehead. Daddy tried his best to keep his cool because he was very protective about his space, and it was obvious that this man had now violated his environment. He began spouting to my father that they were sent by the direct order of the then President, Lyndon B. Johnson. President Johnson was trying to pass laws on the national level that would end the segregation that was still present within our communities, jobs, restaurants, and schools. Two nights prior to the national guards coming to our community, my father said that in July of '67 a black Newark taxi cab driver was murdered by a white man and that's what lead to the riots in our town.

Unfortunately, my generation believes in the practice of an eye for an eye. Even the bible, with some of its glitches, gives references to that notion in Mathew 5:38. There it references loving thy neighbor. What ever happen to the strength in the posturing of non-violence..?

"Sorry, to interrupt you Dr. Neiderbach, but..." the Guard said; while disturbing the tale of my father. She turned to him and said, "Sir, this is a closed session, whatever it is it can wait until I'm done." The guard said, "Is it your request to have more time with your client? If so, I will speak with my superiors and let you know later their decision." He then turned around and left as she looked at me and nodded her head for me to continue the story.

"'Sorry for that Billy, but they should know that when there's a 'do not disturb' sign on the door then they should respect it. As I was about to say, with such detail of your father's life, how do you recall the relation you had with your mother?" asked Dr. Neiderbach.

It was obvious that Dr. Neiderbach was disturbed by the disruption. She really allowed that to bother her. I guess the story of my dad was that moving or maybe she was valuing the time that we were together. Within minutes of the first interruption, that same guard came with three others asking 'Doc' to stand aside and motioning for me to stand. At the time, I didn't know why, what or who they were aiming at, even though it was just the two of us in the room. I slowly looked aside and pointed to my chest saying, "Me?" They just looked at me with a slight surprised look and began moving towards me. For fear of what's to come, I quickly jumped to my feet. The smallest of the guards asked me to turn around with my hands to my front and I obliged without any questions.

CHAPTER 5
Your Honor, Your Honor!

"Wow," was all I could echo as the guard led me through this biggggg room. It was like an auditorium and I was on stage. All eyes were upon me. I could only wonder why. In the crowd were many faces of which some stared with expressions of shock while others wore their sadness. There's Jeannawillis, Martha, Antney and even Albie. I motioned at them to wave but my hands were shackled, preventing me from raising them. As I looked and stared at Jeanna, she quickly turned to the shoulder of her husband, Bobby, and wept. I then formed my lips to ask Albie, "Where's Mommy?" He just bowed his head while wiping the tears from his eyes. The guard pushed me in my lower back saying, "Move it." I somewhat stumbled forward but kept my balance as a big hush rolled through the crowd. I was led to this table where this familiar man stood. He stared back at me while trying to assist me with my balance. He then motioned to the guards to release me of these shackles.

They obliged. I could only thank him for doing me that favor. He must be a friend.

As we sat at the table, Dr. Neiderbach quickly joined us. She asked if I was okay while rubbing me in the small of my back. It felt good to finally have a friendly and familiar touch. I just looked at her and said, "Mame, I feel just fine." She readjusted herself in the chair adjacent to where I sat, pulling on the lapels of her jacket collar. The man next to me leaned over towards me in a calm whisper asking, "Are you feeling better Mr. Bill?" Better than what was all I could think. I was always the one who listened closely to everything that people would say, especially when they're asking me a direct question. I paused before responding and answered him with a question, 'Better than what?' He responded, "The incident that occurred earlier!" Before I could respond, Dr. Neiderbach reached in and told the man, "not now. He's

been through enough for one day."
From that point on I could only wonder
what could have possibly happen to
make him ask me such a question. I
glanced at the papers on the desk, only
to read, '*Jerry Lee Casser, Criminal Defense
Attorney.*'

"All rise, as the Honorable Judge Mary
Nickelson enters the courtroom," was
the strong voice that echoed throughout
the room. Mr. Casser and Dr.
Neiderbach quickly stood as the guard
behind me nudged me to stand. So I
stood. The judge was a rather small-
framed woman with a grave look about
herself. She appeared as if she was in
her mid to early 60s. She sat and began
shuffling the papers on her desk as the
bailiff said, "You may be seated."

From the immediate stare at the judge
and to the area where my family was
sitting, I began to tremor. I could only
wonder what was going on. Martha
slowly motioned her lips say, 'I love

you.' I was comforted knowing that they had seats near me, right over my right shoulder behind the prosecutor so that they could keep a close eye on him. With sweaty palms and trembling legs, Mr. Casser grabbed me by my coattail and told me to sit. For some reason I was petrified. I was completely clueless as to why I was in a courtroom. I kept looking around for more familiar faces, only to find that my family was the only ones present that I knew. The last time I ever remembered my family watching me from afar was when the County honored me as 'Life Saver of the Year' for my heroic duties as an EMT. However, this was strange because for some reason I appear to be the one on trial.

The judge ordered us to stand. She then began asking Mr. Casser if his defendant was ready to proceed with the trial. He looked out at me as to wonder how to best answer the question. "Well, can you give me a moment your honor?" The judge approved. Mr. Casser leaned over to me and said to Dr. Neiderbach, 'how should I best answer that question? Do you think he's able to handle the continuation of this process without blacking out?' The doctor asked, 'what options do we have if you respond no, we're not ready? Would she give us more time?' Mr. Casser turned to the judge and said, 'your honor, your honor, my client has previously experienced another episode of his condition and we feel that he is not fit to stand trail in the condition in which his Psychiatric, Dr. Neiderbach has assessed.

The judge called both, Mr. Casser and the Prosecutor to her bench for a sidebar. I could only wonder what they were talking about. They seemed to be over there talking for a long time. Whatever the conversation was, I only hoped that the results worked in my favor. Suddenly, I began feeling tired, but yet anxious for what was to come. I couldn't control my anxieties nor put ease to my nausea. I feel as if I'm drifting, drifting away….

"Mommy, mommy, please help my mommy!" Mommy and I were getting ready for our ride to her job. My Uncle Glenn and Aunt Florence use to pick us up every day for work. I loved being around my uncle. People use to joke saying that I looked more like him than his own children. Some of my cousins used to call me 'Blackie Jr.' Uncle Glenn was as dark, if not darker than I was. I think I looked just like him, maybe that's why I felt very comfortable being around him. I believe that was the beginning of me having self-esteem issues.

On this particular day, the sky was gray and it had just finished with a slight drizzle. He and auntie had just pulled up in their Gray 1968 Oldsmobile 98, blowing the car horn. Mommy told me to go to the window and see if it was them. 'Mommy, Uncle Glenn is here. He's downstairs with Auntie Flo. Can I go downstairs and tell them that we will be right there?' She told me yes but to also get my raincoat and galoshes before I head down the stairs. I quickly grabbed my coat and climbed onto the banister, as I took to the slide. The banister was our indoor amusement park ride we used to slide the banister from the third to the second and from the second to the first. So off I went. 'Uncle Glenn, mommy said she'll be right down.' He motioned for me to come and get in the car. I was always happy to be greeted by them. Whenever he saw me he would always give me a big piece of candy; so that made the choice to get in easy. I then got in.

As we waited and watched for mommy to come down the stairs, all I could see was Mommy's feet in the air, bag flying, and her blood flowing everywhere.

Slowly she seemed to lose her balance, crashing from the porch and tumbling all the way down to the cement ground, one step at a time. It was like a slow motion flick when you can see every movement and even each grimacing expression of pain. I was helpless, as I watched her fall and felt guilty for once again leaving her side. "Mommy, mommy, please help my mommy" was my cry. Uncle Glenn quickly ran from the car to the bottom of the steps where mommy lied. I soon followed him to be by her side. By the time I got there, her right ankle was twisted back under her left butt cheek. With my selfish self, I could only grab for her to comfort me as she laid there in agonizing pain. Auntie Flo was out the car by that time along with their daughter Louise who also worked with them.

I never wanted to leave mother's side. All I remember, is that I just cried and cried like a baby. I couldn't stand to see her hurt. My only thought was, if she was hurt, who would then take care of me? It wasn't long that my thought became my reality. By the time the local ambulance carrier arrived to take mommy to the hospital, Cousin Louise picked me up and held me in her bosom telling me it's going to be okay. I still cry out, 'mommy, mommy, somebody help my mommy!'

"Billy, Billy, are you okay?" Startled by a forceful shrugging to my shoulder was Dr. Neiderbach calling out my name. I could only wonder if she had lost her mind. She began telling me that I started calling out to someone to help my mother. I could only wonder how she could possibly know what I was thinking about. She then said, 'you're beginning to go into crisis again. I need you to concentrate on happy thoughts. Whatever is going on, don't allow it to distract you from a good feeling. Hey, here's a pad and pen. Do you remember how you would write stories whenever you became anxious and

nervous?' I could only respond, 'yes.'
She then began telling me to write as I
used to write so that I could focus on a
particular task. I could only think about
how I felt, all alone lost within my own
confusion. I felt like a Solitary Man. So
that's when I grabbed the pen and
began writing:

A Solitary Man

Always was he
At a lost for words,
Like that of a mute,
His voice was never heard.

Beaming in his eyes
Were stories never told,
About the life he's lived
That has now become old.

Old, only in the sense
That spoke of the places he'd seen,
That filled his world
With horrible things.

Creeping through his smile
Were those echoes of pain,
That seemed to draw an anger
That constantly poured like rain.

While reaching for help
To understand his past,
He couldn't figure out
Why some friendships never last.

Left only with his heart,
Soul, and pride in his hands,
Here I sit
A Solitary Man!

"How are you making out with your writings Billy," asked Dr. Neiderbach. 'Well I'm fine Doc. Thanks for asking!' She then looked over to see what I had written and I showed her. No sooner than she began reading, Mr. Casser returned to the table. '"What's going on Jerry," asked Dr. Neiderbach. 'Well it appears as if the judge is going to recess us until tomorrow morning 9am. She too thought it was in the best interest of Bill to post-pone this proceeding."

Dr. Neiderbach and I were so excited to know that I wouldn't have to face this judge any longer, at least for the remainder of this day. I was so happy I turned to my family for support, only to see that they all had droopy teary eyes. For the life of me, I thought they would be happy for me. Nonetheless, I was happy, at least for that moment. The guard ordered me to stand and place my hands to my side. As one tightened the shackles around my wrists, the other kneeled to adjust those that wrapped around my ankles. "Let's Go," was their command, "Let's Go!" Jerry asked the guard if we can have two more minutes to finish up and they denied his request. Dr. Neiderbach reached in to hug me, only to be pushed aside with the guard saying, 'We don't have time for that.' As I turned to my family, they were still within their own minds and thoughts. Here I go, that Solitary Man.

As I passed through this long dark corridor, all I could think about is where they're taking me. My fears are no longer present. I think I've finally been lulled by uncertainty that the concerns for my fate have vanished. I used to call for my mother whenever I was afraid, but now it's weird, my pigeons are before me. I keep thinking of how I too can be free. I wanna fly, fly high and far away. Am I stuck in a dream or is this really my reality? "Hey Guard, bring him over to me. A fresh piece of pussy is just what I need." Those echoes of emptiness were soooo far from my mind that had they taken me, it probably would have been better than where I was going.

"Turn Around," said the guard as I motioned towards him. He loosened my shackles and set me free, free to roam a 6 by 9 ft. cell.

Chapter 6
'Drip Drip'

"I got it," was my sigh as I counted each drip that dropped. Drip, Drip, Drip, two, three, four.........sixty. Two, 1, 2, 3, 4..........120. Three, 1, 2, 3, 4...............180. Four, 1........... As each second became a minute and minute became the hour, I laid on this piss filled mattress with just my thoughts. I could only wonder what in the hell was all of that about? Me sitting in a courtroom; My childhood Psychiatrist; An attorney that I don't remember; and most of all, my family sitting in a courtroom crying and looking at me. Where has my life gone?

"Who's there, hey, who's there" was my yell as I sat up from the bed, just so that I could see from where the noise was coming. 'I'm down here. Hey, I'm here. Can you hear me?' I could hear sounds of echoes bouncing off the walls; someone walking and people talking. It's exciting me to no end. I'm feeling so defensive, as if I'm in a fight with an opponent that I can't see. 'Hey, is someone out there,' was my yell. 'Shut the fuck up bitch, you in my motherfucking house now. Why don't you come see……' That must have been that idiot that I passed with the guards on my way in from the courthouse. I pushed my head against the bars, hoping to see if my savior was coming to rescue me from this rat hole. This is weird. I feel as if I'm living vicariously through someone else. 'Shit, it's just the guard!'

"Excuse me Sir, but might you know the time?" He just looked at me and began laughing saying, 'why, you have a date?' I responded, 'no Sir, I just want to know when my friend was coming back to see me.' 'What friend,' he

119

asked? "Dr. Neiderbach, I responded. She was with me before we went to the court earlier.' The guard stopped in his tracks and looked over at me and slowly moved up to the bars that separated us and said with a smirk on his face, 'oh, you that one. I heard a lot about you. You're the family man. Don't worry dude, she probably won't be in here until after shift change, which is in about another 30 minutes or so.' Thanks was all I could say without him seeing me get riled up about his comment. He then continued on his patrol.

For the next 30 or so minutes, I sat back awaiting Dr. Neiderbach to return. I pondered on the thoughts of what he could have meant by saying, 'I heard a lot about you. You're the family man!.' To no avail, his rationale escapes me. I then tried to recall all the events that could have led up until this moment that got me in this situation. For the life of me, my mind continues to draw a blank. I only know that the cell where they were holding me was too small and had a strong uremic stench. The mattress rested on a metal frame of which had no springs, walls were filled with graffiti and writings from every jailhouse poet who thought he had something remarkable to say. In the corner was a sink that constantly dripped. The repetitiveness of the drip could drive anyone insane. Above the sink was a reflective mirror that was made from metal.

As I look at my reflection, I'm shocked to notice that I have smeared blood on the collar of my white shirt, a cut over my right eye, and my mustache is overgrown. Maybe this is why Jeanna and Albie had a hard time staring at me earlier in the courtroom. They know that I'm so vain and I would not be seen looking in any way disheveled. Being in this place made me feel as dirty as one could be. Wanting to feel clean for once, I momentarily stopped the drips by turning on the water facet to splash fresh water on my face.

As I went for my second baptism from the sink water, to my surprise I looked into the mirror and screamed, 'Aaawwwaahhh.' As my vision began to clear, I could see my mother's image reflecting at me. She was still lying there on the ground in a pool of her own blood. 'Mommy, mommy, someone please help my mother. Mommy, it's gonna be okay. I'm sorry. Don't cry. I'm sorry.' I stumbled back over the edge of the bed, still in shock. While rubbing my eyes, her image began to fade. 'Mommy, hold on. Hold on. I hear them coming. Waaaiiitttt!'

Behind me I could hear people talking and walking towards me. The closer they got, the lesser I was able to see Mommy's image. I turned to the bars as to yell for help. To my surprise there stood Dr. Neiderbach and 2 guards.

"Hello Billy, I'm back." While reaching

for my glasses to bring into focus this familiar face, I'm excited to know that my friend has finally returned to rescue me. "Hey Doc, I'm glad you finally made it back. 'Mommy's over here. She needs you. Hurry!'

Without any expression, the guards just opened my cell and told me to stand, turn around and put my arms out to my side as they searched me from head to toe, as if I were some type of criminal. The only time I ever remember being searched like that was when my parents sent me away one summer when I first meet Dr. Neiderbach. "Hey, what are you doing? My mom needs your help."

"Calm down Billy, calm down. She's going to be just fine. Relax." I couldn't understand their lack of urgency to my mother's needs and felt as if they didn't believe me. Only as I pointed to the area of the room where I saw my mother was I too surprised to see mommy wasn't there and that the mirror was smeared with blood. At that point, I could only reassure them that I wasn't crazy and that I did see my mother, after all, her blood is over there.

Dr. Neiderbach motioned to the guards letting them know that I was okay. I heard her whisper to one of them that he was stressing from the events from earlier. Reluctantly the guards obliged her and left the cell. I could see her fidgeting, uncertain on how to approach the situation. Nonetheless, she still looked as beautiful as ever when I got the chance to focus on her once they left us in the cell.

Dr. Neiderbach asked me to sit on the side of the bed because she wanted to talk. I could only wonder about what because of all that has transpired. However, I was so happy to talk again. I remember the last time we spoke. I was in the middle of the story of my father. It was then that the guards interrupted us, ordering us to go into the courtroom. Hopefully we can continue because I didn't really get the chance to tell her all that my dad meant to me, be it good or bad.

"How are you feeling Billy, considering that you had a long day," asked Dr. Neiderbach. 'Well, I'm fine, just a little tired and confused as to what's going on. It just seems as if my life went on this world-wind and I got swept up with it. Doc, can I ask you a question?' She responded, 'yes, ask me anything.' "Well I was wondering, why I keep having bad dreams. A minute ago, I saw my mother lying in a pool of her own blood. It was like she was right over there." Dr. Neiderbach paused for a moment. With what it seemed as if she had tears in her eyes, she reached for my hand and said, "It's going to work out Billy. It'll all be over soon. In the courtroom you exhibited some anxieties when it took Jerry and the Prosecutor a long time to talk with the judge. And that was when I noticed you began calling for help for your mother. If you can remember, it would help you out a lot to write down your thoughts whenever you feel the pressure of your anxieties reaching a peak. Do you think you can do that for me?"

"Well, as you always say, all things are possible. I think I can but it's hard to think to write when your thoughts aren't physical. I will try." She just continued to stroke my hand to offer me more reassurance. Within a split second, Dr. Neiderbach stood up and went to the cell bars, looking down the alley. "Hey Doc, what's wrong," was my question. She responded, 'Nothing,' while rummaging through her bag. Before I could say anything else, she pulls out a small writing pad and an eraserless pencil and says, "Hide this. Tonight's going to be a long night for you in this cell so; I want you to write whatever your thoughts may be when you start to feel nervous or anxious." Quickly I grabbed the pencil and pad and tucked it under my mattress with the intent to follow the doctor's orders.

"Before we were called to the courtroom this morning, we were talking about my father. Can we go back to that story?" She just smiled and said, "As much as I would love to talk more about your dad only, I'm equally curious to hear what you have to say about your parents relationship. How did they meet?"

I knew Doc was asking me a question but I seem to draw a blank and drift, drift away.

"It's been a while since I told the story of how I met my husband. I rememba it like it was yestaday. It was Sunday and ma sista, ma cousin and I had choir rehearsal where I played the piano. That day..."

"Billy, Billy!" Dr. Neiderbach yelled out causing me to look over to her direction. "What are you talking about, Billy? I asked you to tell me how your parents met and then you closed your eyes and started talking in a strong southern accent. What happened to you just now?" I was just as confused as she was. I had no idea of where my mind has just taken me, but I can smell the cigar smoke and alcoholic aroma of where I was about to go. I responded, "I'm not sure Dr. Neiderbach, I think I was my mother, recalling the first time she met my father." She looked at me with a face blanketed with confusion and asked, "Does that happen to you often, where you believe that you are your mother?" I didn't want to answer her but I knew that once she caught wind of something she would be relentless to get her questions answered.

So I said, "My mother and I have always had a special bond. Albie and Antney would say that mommy favored me more than them. Well, she told me a couple of times what she went through to have me. I was what most folks would call a "rough pregnancy."

Knowing, but not understanding it in its entirety and always hearing that I was a *rough pregnancy*, forced me to have a slight resentment towards her. I had no knowledge of what may have happen before I arrived so me now having knowledge of that made me feel as if I was the cause to all of her present day ailments. I would tell her how I always longed for younger brothers and sisters who I could pass things on to. It seemed as if Mommy would tell me about this rough pregnancy story whenever I would bring up the notion of me having a little brother or sister. Well, that day and the entirety of that story would never come to pass. I guess she kept the whole story from me because she may have thought that I was too young to fully understand it. By her not telling me, I always felt as if I was the cause of much pain for her.

My mother, as most people would know her, saw her as a physically challenged person with many years of health issues.

In spite her physical ailments, I always thought of her as the pillar of strength. All of my life, I watched her grimace in pain, she wouldn't utter a word. I watched tears roll down her cheek as her legs swell from a botched surgery. I never told her how much I felt responsible for what she either did with her life or didn't do. Maybe had she told me the story then, I wouldn't have felt that I should have had to take all of the blame for her ailments.

I remember the first day that she told me about my birth. She didn't explain to me the normal birthing cramps or how her water burst. She didn't even tell me how she even got to the hospital. She began describing it to me as an outer body experience. She said it wasn't that she thought she was dead, because she couldn't recount the experience. It was her doctors who told her days later that her heart stopped beating therefore declaring her officially dead.

Mommy later began describing the experience to my dad, grandmother, and the nurse who was taking care of her during that time. Daddy and Granny thought that mommy was hallucinating from her medication because the story she began describing wasn't common. Daddy didn't want her to continue telling this story for fear of his embarrassment of what people may have thought of him. Mommy was very persistent to tell her story. She asked the nurse to summon the doctor who was there. She was determined to revisit that day. Often I think that maybe she may have wanted to act out the scenes in that silent movie to confirm that she was actually the one on the table.

Nonetheless, she told her story by saying that it was as if she felt herself elevated in the corner of the birthing room. She described it as being in a silent movie and not having any parts.

She said that she could see that there was a person on the table but couldn't see the face. Mommy said she didn't hear the "Voice of God" or hear Gabriel's trumpet. "It was a strong ray of light," that she described that seem to pull for her. She said it was like a peaceful place. While yearning to join this light source, she said she somehow looked down towards my grandmother, father, nurses and doctors who were all in the room. She saw Daddy and Granny hugging one another as they cried while the doctors and nurses were doing everything in their powers to resuscitate the image of the woman on the table who was having the baby. Within a split second of seeing Daddy and Granny, mommy said that everything just went black.

Mommy said that as she told her story, Daddy and Granny began to snicker at what she was saying while the doctor and nurses held onto every word. By the end of her story, mommy said that the room was silent and no one made a sound. I guess since outer body experiences were not a popular subject of conversation, it was rare to hear an accurate detail of something that occurred and could accurately be recanted.

Though I don't remember it as vividly as described to me; I was told that I too could have died during this brief moment. She felt as though assuming the risk and leaving her body was her way of giving me a chance to live. From then forward, mommy would tell me this story whenever she thought I was down on my luck and reminding me that we would eternally be connected. It seemed as if she felt all of my pain and happiness because somehow she always knew when I was emotionally struggling.

I then proceeded telling Dr. Neiderbach, "In some ways, I began seeing death as some form of liberation. I think it wasn't until I got older that I was able to understand what it meant to give your life for something greater. Sunday after Sunday we used to go to church to hear about how beautiful and peaceful heaven was. As a kid, I didn't understand all of that afterlife stuff. I didn't know why I cared more for my pets than I did for people. I used to liberate my pigeons once they were injured because I knew that their lives would no longer have value. It amazed me that mommy chose to die, which in turn liberated me. From that day on, I never saw death as a bad thing for anyone or anything suffering from any debilitating ailments. It's a way of being liberated from their pain."

It seemed as if Dr. Neiderbach turned completely pale from what I had just told her, like all of the blood left her body. I got somewhat nervous for her sake, hoping I didn't say anything to discourage her from being my friend. While still appearing alarmed, I slowly walked back to where she was sitting and grabbed her hand. To my surprise, they were wet and had somewhat of a clammy feeling. I said, "Doc, are you okay." It took her a minute to gather her thoughts. She then asked me for something to drink. I was surprised because in this restaurant, there was no service. I then grabbed the first cup I saw which rested on the lid of the sink and tried my best to clean it with just the water. I then filled it and rushed it over to her. "Thank you," was all that she could say while rushing the water down her pipes.

Breathing heavy and with her complexion returning, Dr. Neiderbach tried to compose herself before making any additional comments. I just stood by to assist her with whatever she needed me to do. Just as I thought she was done with asking me questions, out of nowhere her expression went from that of confusion to one of understanding as she tripped over her words saying, "So it seems as if you were even closer to your mother in a spiritual sense! So considering she gave so much for you, how did you feel about her now?"

At first I wondered why she seems to be speaking of my mother in past tense. From this point on, I knew to be cautious with my response to her. Just thinking about my momma caused me to smile at Dr. Neiderbach. I replied by saying, "Before there was God there was my mother. She was the next best thing to him. I never met God in the flesh, or his son Jesus. I only sang songs of how "he touched me." I've read book after book in the bible, but I only understood its meaning through my moms' interpretation. Truly I love the Lord, but I remember most, my mother's touch. It was momma's hands that touched me, her arms that protected me and her love that saved me. Saved me from that whipping my daddy was about to put on me.

Born in the back woods of Virginia some seventy plus years ago, was my mother. She is the youngest of ten children. During that time in the south, many blacks were born poor and into large families. Her parents were sharecroppers. They were the tenants who performed agricultural duties on the land owned by the white family. My grandfather only had a 4th grade education and grandmother never completed the 8th grade. In spite their lack of formal education, my grandparents were determined that their children would receive the best education. Mommy was taught to read at an early age.. Early on when she read, she said that words were like actors and they needed to command the stage. She said that her audience became the characters in each of the books that her older brothers and sisters gave her to read. She believed that her reading could take her to faraway places, places that money could never afford her. She also believed that knowledge would someday lead her to a destiny of liberation.

Momma once told me that her childhood wasn't the best that a child could hope for, but somehow through the love she and her siblings shared brought her through the difficult periods in her life. She never speaks much about the details of her childhood; however, I know she has a story to tell. *I can only hope to be there when she decides to talk.*

Momma is everything to me. She is my hero, love and friend. She's the hope in my dreams, bravery in my spirit and the meaning to my being. It is she who enables me to be here today just to give you insights into my life. Whenever I think of my mother, she best reminds me of a mixture of Sisters Betty Shabazz and Maya Angelou, they both share a strong physical resemblance to my mother. From the broadness of her hips and the flaring of her nostrils, momma along with Sisters Betty and Maya breathe life into those of us who they can in contact with. Her appearance is stereotypical of what a strong black mother would represent. Momma's stout in stature with draping shoulders, childbearing hips, skinny free and most of all her face is painted by the wrinkles that are expressionistic of her life stories.

Spiritually, she possesses the sound silence that only tragedy and triumph teaches. Often without question, she has become a counselor to all hoping to seek guidance through a tunnel called religion. She'll quietly lead you from that tunnel into your own awareness. Claiming none, but accepting all, she'd unselfishly share in her convictions. Her patience is long and enduring, usually for the children that she carried during their journeys into infancy. Compromising her own body for the safety of her children, she has welcomed me into a safe haven called life. She is my woman, strong, black, full-figured and haughty, who is not ashamed to be woman. Her femininity has taught me most of what it means to be a man. I owe all that I have and am to her. She owns this body, mind and spirit. However beautiful, bold or strong, she is the caretaker of me."

Dr. Neiderbach says, "That's very interesting Billy. It seems as though your mother also had a rather vivid imagination that allowed her to also mentally drift to other places. What an incredible development, Billy!" Dr. Neiderbach began writing into her notepad while quietly jotting the many thoughts from her head. I was hoping she would understand how I feel about my mother. While finishing up her last sentence, she looks up at me saying, "Now Billy, can you take me back to where we started this conversation by letting me know how your parents met."

My face beamed with excitement as I said, "It's a funny story how my parents met. I always told them that their story was one for the books. My mother, who is the youngest of her siblings, was being raised by an Aunt up north in New Jersey. As you know, with many of those large black southern families, members were sent north hoping to get better jobs and education in the desegregated north. Well, this particular aunt was her father's older sister. She was a Devout Pentecostal Preacher who was heavily involved in this large church movement called the Zion Mission. This organization appeared to be a cult to most who didn't understand the Pentecostal denomination. To most, it appeared to be the breeding ground for many of those fiery, heaven bound, no color wearing, strict holy rolling preachers. So, with mommy and her siblings being raised under her guidance, they became very active in the church. Mommy played the piano, taught Sunday School,

and became a member of the YPHA-
Young People Holy Association.

One day she, two of her sisters and their
cousin decided to take the long way
home from church. This particular
route was preplanned. Her cousin
Louis knew of a clubhouse and was
raving about it called the Piccadilly
Club, located on Peshine and Waverly
Avenues. At this club, talented singers
would perform and folks from all over
would swing dance throughout the
night. So on this day, mommy's sisters
hid other outfits underneath their
clothes. They didn't want to look like
the sanctified sisters that they were. So
they all wore attire fitting for an older
woman who was about to hit the club as
opposed to the teenage girls they were.
My mother had no clothes to change
into so she was forced to doll up her
makeup and hike up church skirt, but
was too uncomfortable to remove her
sweater and glasses.

They got dressed, well…, that's to say undressed and prepared in the alleyway behind the clubhouse, while hiding their change of clothes in a bag next to the rear of a dumpster. As mommy would say, *"Our excitement was unexplainable as we approached the long line."* She continued to say that, "with every step closer to the entrance, I was able to hear one of the sweetest voice I've ever heard singing a rendition of my favorite song, 'O Danny Boy.' I couldn't wait to go inside. The room was so loud and smoky. The men were all wearing fancy suits while the women wore corset style dresses with lots of pearls. I looked around to see where the voice was coming from and that's when I locked eyes with this rather short stranger who was wearing a fancy suit with an even fancier bow tie. He had slicked back hair and appeared to only be singing to me. He began to sing the lyrics with more passion as he started to walk over to where we were standing. He couldn't have been looking at me; he must have been looking at my older sister who was standing right beside me with her chest spilling out the top of her dress. Yet, it was like he never took his eyes off of me. He approached us and grabbed my hand and sung the rest of the song right to me. I looked over to my sisters and cousin and they were showing green eyes. Ha, ha, who would have thought a man would come up to me before either of them.

After he finished singing the song he walked the microphone back to the stage and came back over to us while the next person began to perform. He came and introduced himself and told me how beautiful I was. I didn't realize what he really saw in me til some six years later and five little ones to feed. Nonetheless, I couldn't stop blushing as he continued with his compliments. The only thing that I can say is that I started to feel a spark for him. Never has anyone shown me such attention, especially before my sisters. My sister who was very protective of me grabbed my hand and said it was time for us to go. The singer who was infatuated with me ordered my sisters and my cousin some drinks and said he just wanted to talk to me at one of the tables for a few minutes. The thought of some drinks excited them but she warned him to remain in sight so she can keep an eye on him. He was a perfect gentleman leading me by my hand and escorting me to the table. We talked there for what seems like an hour just learning about each other."

Later I asked my father how he felt about mommy when he first met her. He never seemed to give a straight answer. He said that he thought she looked very innocent. It was her innocence that attracted him to her, as he thought she would be an easy conquest. At that time I wasn't sure what he meant by that, it wasn't until I was older when I finally understood the meaning.

From that moment on, both of their lives would be changed forever. Less than a year later my mother was forced to tell her father and his sister, the Preacher, that she was pregnant. Growing up in a religious household this was something she was dreading to do. Usually, in that time, your family and the church would arrange the person you were to marry. So telling her father what she has done, came with a harsh backlash because of the multiple disappointing aspects of the situation. My father knew that he would have to put his career and political fight on hold to start his transition into fatherhood. So he did just that, stopped rallying votes and even stopped performing. He wanted to do right by us and didn't want to have a reputation for having children outside of wedlock. So in September of 1960, they had a quick in home wedding with only immediate family in attendance. If you look at the wedding photos you can unwittingly tell she's at least 3 months pregnant.

Life for them began to get harder as time went on causing my father to have to find more work while my mother seemed to get pregnant each and every year. If ever my dad or mom for that matter thought that they would have a storybook ending to their romance, well I'm sure both would agree not. My dad began to belittle my mother and she began to lose confidence in her appearance and self esteem. Those hips that attracted most men with that small waistline vanished. Rather than allow the negativity to keep her down, mommy said that she just redirected all of her energy into us. She loved to nurture us, to care for us to make sure we were always taken care of. It was like my father brought in the money and momma took care of everything else. She was our superhero and whenever Daddy would come home upset and try to take it out on the kids she would swoop in and save many of butts from being whipped that night."

Dr. Neiderbach says, "It seems like you've got a lot of the qualities your mother use to possess. I can see why you were so close. How was it as a child for you growing up in that environment?" I didn't immediately respond to her question because my thoughts were still focused on mom. It was then that I stood up and walked over to the sink, cupped my hand and took a sip of water. I got thirsty talking so much of mine and my mother's experiences. Doc's eyes just followed me as I quenched my thirst. With a soft voice I heard her ask, "Do you still remember any of your writings from your childhood?" I just wiped my mouth dry with my hand and began reciting "Shattered Dreams."

Chapter 7
Echoes of my Dreams

Ancestrial Talk

Never forget those thick hot shackles
That burned my neck, wrists, and ankles,
Until it brightened my color.

Never forget the sharp pains
That I endured with every slap of the whip
Across my blistered back.

Never forget those wet chilly nights
That accompanied me
To the outhouse every evening.

So never forget
Why I suffered so much
So that you could read this that I write

So please, never forget!

Dr Kneiderbach took to her pen, as if she didn't want to forget any thoughts or occurrences of our experience in this cell. In deep thought she wrote while periodically glancing over her glasses. I could only wonder what she was writing about. The most I got out of her at that time was just a quick glance. Before long, all of her attention was back on me. I was hoping that she would be able to handle whatever answers I had to the questions she presented me with.

For a minute I thought our session was over. It's been over 2 hours that the guards allowed us to talk. As much as I'm enjoying this time together, I know that it's too will soon end. I could hear in the distance the guards talking to other prisoners telling them that they only had ten more minutes before this cell block is on lockdown. Therefore, our time together is nearing its end.

"Excuse me Doc, I think the guards are telling everyone that they have to leave soon." She quickly responded, "yeah I do hear them. Considering we are heading back to court in the morning, I will fight for an extension on my time with you. So, let's not focus on them any longer. I want you to know that I appreciate everything you said about your mom and the events surrounding her outer body experience, but in order for me to help you William, I need you to go back to your childhood and tell me more about your relationships with your siblings, things you did for fun, and your friends and pets."

If my past should have taught me anything, it's that I can't sneak anything by her. When I used to visit her office as a young man, I would try to tell deceptive stories just to pass the time I had to spend with her. Initially, I didn't like going to visit her, but her charm eventually grew on me. It was the state that forced me to see her from the start; at least that's what I heard. There was something about her that she could always see right through me, right through all of my bull. She really took the time to understand me. Out of everyone that I know, past and present, I can truly say that she knows me well. Therefore, I feel compelled to tell her the rest of my story in all honesty.

"Okay, Dr. Neiderbach, when I was younger, one of the games that we use to play that ended up giving us broken bones was roof hopping." She looked at me in disbelief and asked, "Roof Hopping?" With a crooked smile I replied, "Yes, Roof hopping." I began tell her that often we would chance each other at which one of us had the most heart to jump from our roof to or neighbors house three story up from the ground.

One day while in the hot sun, Jeannawillis, Albert, Antney, Jack and his sisters Lina and Tricia and myself decided to have a little fun. Fun for us meant many things. On this particular day, the guys were always consciously proving to the girls which one of is had the most nerves, whether is was the game Truth or Dare, Catch a Girl Kiss a Girl, or just Roof Hopping. We just had great times. Our method of proving who had the most nerves was to be the first one to jump from one rooftop to the next house. This was about my only opportunity to not be showed up by my two older brothers. Even though they were older, I believe that I possessed a more natural athletic ability. This only meant to me that I would have to be the one to chance the first and jump over to Mrs. Codney's roof first before either of them.

As I looked around, all of the boys were on our rooftop gathering up the nerve as to what they were going to do once they got over to Mrs. Codney's roof. The girls were standing around in their circle of sisters blushing and looking over at the boys. I guess they too were wondering which one of the boys they wanted to kiss. I on the other hand was so stupid and naïve that all I could think about is how fast I could cross the 4ft space without plummeting thirty feet to the ground. Even though I was usually the first one over, more often than not, I was the first sent back because they viewed me as the little kid. To be honest, that didn't bother me that they would send me back because my goal was to be the one over so that I could get a feel of either of the sisters. A feel was all that I needed, I didn't need any more than that at the time. To put things in perspective, Lina and Tricia were the neighborhood hot mommas. Every guy in the neighborhood wanted them. However, we were the fortunate ones to live next door to them so we were afforded the extra luxuries of seeing them after-hours.

One incident that always comes to mind when I think back to how we would jump from one rooftop to the next was when my mom and Mrs. Codney were in the window talking. It was routine for us to check out whether they were in the window before we would jump the rooftops. For some reason, all of us must have been still excited from the earlier game of hide n seek, that we just forgot to make sure that the windows were vacant. As I remember, Albert beat me across the roof to their house. He never looked down nor back as to see what we were doing or just to take a glimpse at the window to ensure its vacancy. After Albert jumped, Antney surely followed him to the Codney's roof. Jack shortly afterwards joined our roof where Jeanna and me were still standing.

I began to get so jealous at watching my brothers with Lina and Tricia that I just took off into the air, across to their

rooftop. At the time, I didn't have a care
in the world other than to get a little
attention from those sisters. So, as I
leaped into the air between the two
buildings with my hormones raging like
wildfire, something told me to look
down. As I took a little peak to see
whatever I could, my mother and Mrs.
Codney were almost falling out the
windows with disbelief that we were
jumping from one rooftop to the next.
Man, I didn't know what to do. As soon
as I landed, I fell at Lina's feet. I was so
scared; I didn't know how to land...
From that point on, I could care less
about those sisters. Albert came over to
me with Tricia at his side and picked me
up and asked if I was okay. The only
thing that I could say at the time was,
'they saw us, they saw us!' Albert,
Tricia and Lina looked at me and asked,
'Who saw us?' I said, 'MOMMY! They
were in the window!' No sooner than I
said that, I looked over at our rooftop
and saw Jack stammering at our
bedroom window while Jeanna stood

there motionless and crying. As I remember, Antney leaped into the Codney's girl's bedroom window, forgetting the fact that he doesn't live there. Lina and Tricia immediately followed behind him. Albert and I stood to await our fate. We knew that we couldn't go into the Codney's house because they had Mickey, a mean German Shepard.

Albert then told me not to talk. 'Don't say a word. Leave all the talking up to me.' Albert knew that once I was scared I would squeal like a pig. As we saw two adult male hands reached out from inside the window, we now knew why Jack was stammering like never before and Jeanna was crying. It was my father. What he lacked in height, he made up for it in brutality.

'Oh God, Oh God,' was all I could say. I knew that this was the end to my life. My dad had a way of beating us like no other. If there was one thing that I feared most, it was my dad and what he was capable of doing to me. My knees began shaking, heart began to thump, tears just flowed down my face, I was scared, scared as hell. As I looked over at Albert, he was uncontrollably chewing his fingernails to the very nubs. He seemed to be hungrier than anything. Daddy then stuck his head out the window. With pain and anger written all over his face, he tried to hide it and coax us to safety. I made this jump a million times before, but with him present, I couldn't move. My feet felt like they were glued to the tarred roof. He knew that I was afraid of him and if he was to motion me the wrong way, no telling what my fate would have been. It took Albert to hold me to get me to jump back to our roof. When I got to the window, all I heard my father say he gently pulled me in the window, 'It's O.K! Son, it's OOOOOO KAY!' Well I need not tell you that day wasn't the first nor last of a long history of beatings, one of which my other finger was broken.'

"Billy, did I hear you correctly? You previously mentioned how he broke your finger before? Did you say your father broke your finger again, " Dr. Neiderbach asked with a startled voice. "Yes'm" I replied, "He showed his love for us in that manner on many occasions. He would tell us that he beat us because he loved us that much. "What happen after he saw your finger broken this time?" I paused for a moment before answering her because she seem to want to blame my dad for everything. I felt that what happen was so long ago and it seemed as if she was trying to go back to that space. To me, my dad and I settled that score years ago so going back into that time would probably make me mad.

She looked at me patiently awaiting my answer. I told her that he said, 'Now it's YOUR wings that are clipped, and hopefully for your sake, I won't catch you flying high again across that roof again!' All I could do from that point on was just wait until my Mother came to my rescue." I knew with my mother, all I had to do was cry as loud as I could before long she would wander from where she was to aid in my rescue.

Dr. Neiderbach was shocked, all the years I've been visiting with her, never once did I told her about the degree of abuse my siblings and I had to endure. I was in no way surprised at her reaction. I felt that it was my job not to throw my siblings under the bus. If they didn't want to talk about their pains at the hands of daddy, then it wouldn't be me to expose it. Even when I mentioned the story of how my finger got broken before, I told her as if it was my fault.

"Has he ever displayed this anger to anyone outside of your immediate family?" she asked. I took a deep breath as I leaned back a bit, "My father was never shy about letting you know how he felt about things; he would flaunt his views as if it were a new car. Daddy for the most part had two different personalities. He had the playful teddy bear while hiding the angry monkey that rode on his back. He turned both on like a light switch.

One time one of my favorite cousins Trent came by our house to stay with us over the weekend. His part of the family was better off than ours. I think he enjoyed just being around more down to earth people who were less stuck up. Either that or it's because he knew my brothers and I were Dare Devils and he wanted to take a walk on the wild side. One weekend when he came over, he brought some firecrackers and a box of stick matches. This was the first time I have ever been around any type of explosives and I was excited to get my hands on them. Trent, Albie and I all ran to my room as we were planning to go to the roof to throw them off the side of the building as people walked by. That was the plan until Trent said, 'U know what we should do? We should put the fire crackers in a pot so won't no one get hurt if they happen to walk by it will make the sound louder."

Albie was quick to jump on that idea, but I was not as enthused. See our father was home asleep and he hated to be awaken. Furthermore, I didn't want to be held responsible for waking him up. Nevertheless Trent handed me the matches and Albie the fireworks. He thought that by doing that we could only use them together. Albie told me to wait in my room so I wouldn't make any noise while Trent showed him which was a good pot to use. I didn't want any part of waking up my father so instead of putting up a fight to go with them like I usually would, I just complied.

They left the room and I just stared at the box of stick matches, I held it by the side and poked the center slowly out. Then I began to count the matches, there were sixteen in total. **CRASH! BANG! RATTLE!!!** *'Who dat makin aw dat noise in dat kitchen!?'* Ut-Ohh, Daddy's up. I quickly flew out to see to make sure Trent and Albie were okay. I got there before my father was able to get out the bed and I asked them what happen. It seems Trent tripped with the pot in his hand. My father screamed out, *'Who dat in the kitchen*!?' This time with a horrific voice that gave us all goose bumps. It was as if God himself was speaking directly to me.

On the other hand, my brother Albert always seemed to be the one with the most heart. When my dad asked the question, Albert responded for Trent. I really don't think he feared anyone. Sometimes I'd wonder if something was really wrong with him or if he was just acting crazy. I never even pondered the notion that he may have had my sister Jeannawillis' ailment, a dying commitment to protecting a younger brother. Well, when it came to me, to hell with that stuff. Albert and Jeannawillis could protect me any day of the week and twice on Sunday. I wasn't trying to be a super hero and speak up for nobody, not even myself. I guess this was one of the major differences between Albert and myself at that time because he would always speak up for someone else whether they were right or wrong. So it wasn't surprising to me that he ran to Trent's aid and told my dad that it was he who was in the kitchen.

You should have seen the expression of relief on Trent's face. He had no clue as how to handle the situation that he now found himself in. Luckily, Albert runs to my daddy's bedroom, and Trent and I quickly followed him only to the door. As I peaked around the corner to see and hear what Albert was about to say my Daddy, sweat began running down my brow. I guess you can say that I was nervous as hell and sweating like a pig. All at once, my hands and knees began shaking for fear of what my dad would do to him. I was also somewhat embarrassed because Trent was now present to witness how Daddy would often express his love to us.

He, along with many of our relatives used to tease us about how our father would beat us at the drop of a dime. I remember being sooo embarrassed whenever they laughed at the fact that we got beatings and their parents didn't. I always knew that he would one day have his opportunity with Daddy. I just didn't know it would be today. As I looked over at him, he too was shaking. Now grant it, I feared my dad for good reasons, but I couldn't understand why Trent had so much fear of him. I guess those stories that others told about us finally landed in his lap. In spite Trent's teasing, I didn't know he feared him until I noticed he was standing in a puddle of his own piss. I looked at Trent with disbelief. I couldn't believe that he would allow himself to do something like that. I began trembling and stammering while looking at him, but not loud enough for my dad to hear us. Trent got so embarrassed, he ran into the bathroom right pass my dad, with a trail of water streaming from his pants leg. I really felt bad for him and I really didn't want to make him feel any more embarrassed than he was already feeling. Trent must have thought that something cruel was going to happen to me, Albert or maybe to him. I guess not knowing something is just as bad as knowing.

While I listened to Albert and my father, I noticed that Albert was just telling my dad and old lie. He told him that he was only in the kitchen trying to find his G.I. Joe's shirt. He even told my dad that I told him it was in the pantry and that was why he heard the pans banging. I couldn't believe that Albert could just create his own stories under such pressure and furthermore, include me in it. When I think about it, he should have been a lawyer because my dad believed every word that he said or least we thought he did.

After hearing what Albert had to say, my dad only ordered him to prepare him something to eat. Now that was a surprise. Usually if you disturbed my father's rest, he'd always let you know just how much it meant to him. Daddy never asked you to do something for him, it was always an order. I guess that goes back to his military days of receiving orders from the big man. Albert then ran out of my dad's room in great relief to fulfill my dad's order. I'm sure that he surprised himself he was able to pull that one off for Trent. Motionless I remained on the wall as Albert left the room, frozen from the shock that he was able to get away without having to be harshly punished.

His confidence was so high that he even gave me a big high five. 'Man, that was a relief!' he said. I was still too nervous to move. I barely gave him the high five. I don't think my hand went any further than my waist. In retrospect, that incident and others forced me to have a greater appreciation for Albert because of his willingness to always look after someone who may be in need."

"So Billy, would it be fair to say that your brother Albert came to your rescue a lot." Dr. Neiderbach said. I replied by saying, "He sure did. He was like my Knight in shining armor." "That's great that he was there for you and your father wasn't able to act as harshly as before. Was that the last time Trent visited? She asked. "In spite of that experience, Trent never stopped coming to our house. I truly believed he loved his cousins in a special way after that situation. He would come over almost every other weekend; that is until the last time…" I stopped my sentence there. I didn't want to explain any further, but she noticed, like she always does as she asks, "What last time? Don't hold anything back, I'm here to help." So I continued.

"The last time Trent stayed the night at our house, my momma came home in tears. My father who was watching T.V. on the sofa quickly ran to aide his crying wife. Trent and I were just playing in my room we heard the commotion. We quickly rushed down to see what happened, but seeing my mother in that manner was hard for me to bear and I started crying too. This was the first time my father didn't scorn me for crying. He just continued to console my momma as he asked her what was wrong. She told us that her Boss fell into a coma after a car accident on his way to work and his family decided to pull the plug on him rather than allow him to fight for his life. Once my father heard this, his sympathy turned into dismissal. My father said, 'You gotta be kidding me, that has you upset? Come on Hun, you know there's no fear in death and that it's a better life waiting on the other side. His family just didn't want him to suffer any longer in this life.' She replied, 'I know, dat ain't all, they closed da office down and laid off everyone. 'The bills are due, the insurance's due, everything's due. We have no extra money now.' She continued to cry out louder and louder and so did I. I had to run out the room because I just couldn't be there anymore. I ran to my room and set down on the floor. I closed my eyes. Darkness… Silence… I was finding peace until Trent came in my room screaming, 'Bill-lllyyy, wat ya doin wit dat bird in your hands.' I opened my eyes, looked down at my hands and saw a bloody pigeon head in my left hand and his body half in my right. To this day I can't recall what happened, but will never forget the look on Trent's face when he discovered me. He had the look of confusion and terror and I could not explain.

We ended up going to bed almost right afterwards. I don't remember lying in the bed but I remember hearing Trent snoring. All I could think about was what my father told my mother and what she told him about the money, or lack thereof. I knew there had to be something I could do, but didn't know what it was. I continued to fly through the randomness of my thoughts and I started to feel this cool breeze against my face and this feeling that I was ascending to a higher elevation. It was as if my mind and body had separated and I had no control. Where was my body taking me? I had no idea, but there was no way I could fight it. My eyes were shut but somehow I can see the excitement surrounding me. Now the air is hitting my skin at a faster rate as it seems I am now descending. 'What is that warmth?' I wondered but I couldn't get my eyes to open to find out what it was. It felt as if I was right next to the sun. Then I heard my father's voice, this time it wasn't scary, but more like he was scared. 'Billy, wake up boy. Wake up!' He said. I woke up to find myself outside the house right below the fire escape. In my hands was a frightened Flappie who was snuggled between my forearm and my chest. I look at my family and everyone was crying. My mother, father and my siblings were all hysterical and I didn't know why; until I turned around and saw our home on fire. 'Where's Trent!' I yelled out, but no one responded. My mother just grabbed me, held me close and said, 'He's in a better place now.' I didn't fully understand at first so I asked, 'Did he go back to his house?' She just squeezed me closer as she cried in my arms and said, 'He didn't make it out...' He didn't make it out..."

Chapter 8
'The day after'

There's a great force that is lifting me.
I'm powerless, but yet, I feeling
comforted. "Guard, Hey Guard, get me
a…!" It's a voice coming straight from
the heavens. It sounded as if it was from
my beautifully winged Angel. There's a
breeze, a soft fresh breeze brushing
against my body. I know this feeling
from before. I'm once again in flight. In
spite my clipped I'm flying on my own.
These wings have finally healed for me
to fly again; fly, fly high and free. I can
see the heavens before me. There's my
next destination. 'Beep, Beep, Beep.'
The sounding beeps are causing me to
rapidly descend, forcing my heart to
race. I closed my eyes for fear of my fast
ending approaching. Will this be my last
trip? I'm all alone. I'm scared. My blue
skies have now turned white. As I

opened my eyes I'm now surrounded by white walls and beeping noises. I hear voices and see images through my blurred vision.

"Bill-lllyyy, Bill-lllyyy, you finally woke up, how are you feeling?" I looked to my right to see and there's my friend Dr. Neiderbach standing beside me. I go to reach for her but my distance is restricted due to restraints around my wrist. "Doc, how did I get here?" I asked. She looked at me with eyes of both confusion and compassion. I didn't remember the events leading to me being in a hospital room, I mean how could I, that's probably why instead of having me figuring it out on my own, she did something I never seen her do before and that's confide in me. She said, "this is the first time in 25 years of practicing have I ever been so scared for a patient. One minute you were telling me a story about your cousin and your childhood the next minute you had blood pouring from your eyes before you collapsed on the floor and began to seizure. I was so worried about you; I haven't left your side since you were rushed to the infirmary. They still haven't discovered the cause for your Haemolacria or the cause for your convulsion but they're currently running some tests and should be back soon with the results. I still can't believe what I witnessed, I'm just glad you're awake now. Hopefully you'll feel better in the morning."

From everything she just told me the only thing I was the most concerned with is that she said I will get transferred back to the cell sometime in the middle of the night. So I asked, "I thought you said that we were going to court in the morning?" Her eyes went from me to glaring at the floor as she says, "Billy you have been unconscious for over 5 hours, we don't have much time now, but we need to pick up with our session. That's the only way I can help you." My mind was in circles. First

I wake up handcuffed to a hospital bed then I find out I missed a whole day talking to this fine white woman.

Dr. Neiderbach was a rather peculiar looking woman. She stood around 5'6" and weighed somewhere around 150lbs. She wasn't the snazziest dresser that one would expect. She seemed to be from the hippie day; listening to some folk music while smoking a fat joint. I think I became so mesmerized by the fact that she was the first white woman that I had ever seen with an afro. I mean an afro. Her afro may have attracted my attention first, but shortly it became the gentleness of her voice that cushioned my soul. She lulls me into her zone and relaxes me.

I should have been thinking about the cause for my condition but I was more concerned with time missed. I hate to miss time, time is the one thing you can lose but never get back, so I never liked to waste it. Which reminds me of the phrase "Funny how times fly" because it can mean so much depending on the interpretation. One thing that comes to mind is the first pigeon I found as a child which I was told would never take flight again and how with time he one day flew. They say that a broken wing bird will never fly. Somehow, he got away from me, just as time, escaped my grasp. It really is funny how time flies.

A white flash gets my attention as I look over and see a man in a white lab coat leaving the room slamming the door behind him. I scroll back to Dr. Neiderbach and ask, "What was he doing here?" She looked at me with confusion as she says, "The doctor just stood here and checked your vitals and asked you questions to check your coherency which you responded to. He said your test results came back negative for any physical ailments, but neurologically... Have you ever been in a car accident or taken a fall when you were younger?"

I had no idea what one thing happening to me while I was younger would have anything to impact as to why I was here, but I responded anyway. "Yes'm, one time when me and my brothers were walking to school, we noticed a ladder on the ground between two car garages that were space at least two car lengths apart. We placed the latter to the rear of one of the garages. My brother Antney decided he wanted to go roof hopping since we have never jumped something with that distance; he wanted to be the first of us to go. I really didn't want to try it because I was the smallest and didn't think I would make it. That was before I was leaping with the best of them, but that didn't stop my brothers; so I went along.

Albert went first and made it with ease, still wearing his book bag. Antney soon followed him but his landing wasn't nearly as smooth. His right leg was dangling off the edge and he had to pull himself up with his left and Albert's hat. They began to egg me on for me to jump so I mustered up the courage. I figured if they both made it with their book bags on; if I toss mine over before I jump I should make it with no problem. That's exactly what I did, I took my book bag off and tossed it to Albie. Antney began to tease me calling me a baby for taking my bag off. I was enraged so I took to flight right off the roof with no running start as I leaped. I looked to for my landing and saw nothing but wall. *Splat* I hit the side of the garage and fell right to the driveway. Luckily for me, a young Paramedic was driving by and saw my fall and quickly ran to my aid. They say I was out for about five minutes before he actually showed up, but to me it seems almost instant."

Dr. Neiderbach was more concerned now, then I have ever seen her before and she asks, "Do you remember what the doctors told you and was there any changes after that fall, that you noticed?" I replied, "Actually I never went to a doctor, the Paramedic said I appeared fine except for a lump on my forehead. He wanted me to go to the hospital for tests but older brother somehow persuaded him not to take me. Which is something I'm grateful for, because if my father would have found out how I got injured, I might have been worse off then I already was. In that situation I'm not sure who the real hero was, my brother or the Paramedic. After that accident I became more adventurous and willing to be the first to do anything risky. I became more social, creative and had a desire to help people like the Paramedic who helped me. I figured that the fall if anything empowered me to do everything because a month later we went back and I made it."

Her face said that she was impressed; but her words were saying, "I'm not sure but that may have been the cause for the damages the doctor found in your frontal lobe, if you would have gone to the hospital you might have been diagnosed and treated." "What do you mean I have damages? Still? From when I was a child?" I asked. She said, "It's possible but I don't know for certain, but it seems too relative. I'll raise a scenario to ask the doctor if that's a possibility. You mentioned a Paramedic having an influence on you; didn't you once spend time as a Paramedic or EMT?"

Before I replied, I took a moment to look around the room, familiarizing myself with a scene I once knew. Then said, "Yes, I was a Paramedic and I drove around in an ambulance with an EMT, being in this room reminds me of the year I worked both the ambulance and the ER. I was really devoted to helping people and spent almost all my time doing so. That year it was extremely busy, the hospital was getting flooded

185

with victims of gun violence, fires and heart attacks.

During that year, one week in particular I saved over thirty lives single handedly. It started when we were called out to a fire where a home was ablaze and the fire department has already been dispatched. What was unusual was that somehow I arrived at the fire before everyone, even my own partner; I was able to pull out a family of four which included a mother and her three kids. I went back for the screaming voice in the back room, but there was too much smoke for me to take and I had to run back out the house. That's when I was grabbed by my partner and he attempted to wrap me in a blanket. I resisted as I yelled for someone to go save the person who was still in the house. The fire department was more concerned with connecting their hose and containing the fire then going in to save the person who was left inside.

I don't remember what happened after that or how I got there for that matter but I know I had to talk to my supervisor right after. As I stood in the hall waiting to be called in, I began to fiddle with the objects in my pocket and searched for the box of matches Trent gave me as a child. Whenever I got nervous about something I would reach for that box and just hold it, count the matches. It reminds me of a time of peace.

'Billy, come in here!' The sound of my supervisor Mr. Clark's voice startled me almost causing me to drop the matches but I was able to keep control of them and quickly get them back in my pocket. I walked into his office and he was all smiles congratulating me on a job well done. There was something he said that will always stick with me, 'I'm not sure if I should be praising you or questioning how you were the first on sight for three different fires in the area with absolutely no explanation, but this decision is above me.' Then I was offered the opportunity to work in the hospital which I gladly accepted.

I went home that day and prepared to get some rest for the next workday and while I was undressing the matches fell out my pocket. After Mr. Clark startled me I never got a chance to put them back in the box but I made sure I didn't drop any on the floor. I counted them as I put them back in the box and there were eleven in total. That's when I got a phone call saying there was a shootout and they need extra hands in the ER so I flew over there as quick as possible.

I arrived at the hospital and there were bloody victims everywhere; I quickly prepped and started assisting the doctors with the patients. One patient who I tended, had three gunshot wounds one from a .38 Caliber in his right shoulder and two self inflicted wounds to his stomach from a .357. The patient was losing a lot of blood and one of the bullets had pierced his lung so he had to be attached to a breathing a machine. There was something about this guy that reminded me of my cousin Trent and I just wanted to make sure he was ok, so I paid close attention to his recovery.

Next thing I know I'm walking through the halls and I'm stopped by a woman that says, 'Sorry to stop you, I'm sure you're busy saving lives, but I had to thank you for saving mine. You rescued me and my three sons when our house caught on fire in the middle of the night.' I sadly replied, 'I'm sorry I couldn't do more to save the person left in the house. I really felt bad about that." With tears in her eyes she said, 'don't worry yourself about that, you saved four lives that night and we're grateful. The person who was left was my sick elderly grandmother who we were helping and I was working three jobs to take care of her medical needs along with the everyday needs of the family. They say God has a plan and I truly believe that. It was in his plan because through her death, we were blessed with a Life Insurance Policy as well as a settlement from the insurance company. It will have us in a new more secure home and I'll be able to spend more time loving my children. You gave my family another chance and we're forever indebted.' Hearing this actually made me feel better and opened my eyes to something that should have been clear all along as I gave her a modest smile and said, 'you're welcome, I was just doing my job. What brings you in here today; is everything okay?' Her mood quickly switched and she said, 'no, my son was one of the people shot in today's shooting at the store. He was just getting some milk for his little sisters and the guy walked in the store and shot everyone, that's when the store owner shot him in the shoulder and he shot himself in the side. I hope he burns for the pain he's caused people, the pain he has caused my son who may never walk again.' I couldn't believe what she was telling me, the guy I was trying to save was the reason everyone was there in the first place. Only thing I could say was, 'I'll personally look after your son to make sure he recovers.'

I don't remember leaving that lady but I do remember seeing myself in that guy's room. Staring at him; listening to the rhythm of the machines beeping for his heart and inhaling/exhaling for his lungs. It was almost poetic until all of a sudden it just stopped and I closed my eyes as silence filled the room. Three minutes later a beep sounded as a long pause rang, as to say, the end. When I opened my eyes back up I was on the roof top tending to my birds.

I have rescued and collected over 20 pigeons by this point, some were injured prior to my appearance, however, more than most were injured after my emergence but I tend to them the same nevertheless. I can really feel free when I'm surrounded by my birds, with not a care in the world. I would sit on the edge of the roof with a few of my favorite birds on my lap and just stare out into the sky and dream of one what it would be like to truly be free amongst the heavens, to fly higher than any bird. To be amongst the angels like the people whom I helped save."

Dr. Neiderbach interrupts and says, "So you were sort of like a hero, right for man and pigeons. What did you mean by, 'injured after you emerged' and the people who you saved being angels?" "Well, sometimes you're lucky enough to find a pigeon that's been injured and other times you see that the bird needs your help but doesn't know it so you have to, in a way, bring it to their attention that you're needed. The same went for families I helped," was my reply. She just wore a look of shock before saying, "That's a very interesting take on things; tell me more about the people you saved."

I continued where I left off and said, "I was really on a role with saving and freeing lives when my work got the attention of the superiors once again. This time it was more of a negative experience because Mr. Clark and two other executives questioned me about the amount of people who were dying in areas that I was seen working in. They wondered if I was being neglectful to the patients. After no conclusion was reached they decided to suspend me until the investigation was over.

"Bill-lllyyy," Dr. Neiderbach called out. "Did you write anything in your diary about how it made you feel?" I paused for a moment and then I recited to her what I had written:

Shatter Dreams

Shattering glass,

It fell from my window pane,
Crumbling to the floor,
One misty summer night.
(A gloom sight)

Pouring drops,
From the rain that fell,
Wet my floor,
Sopping the dust from the corners.
(Cleaning the borders)

Dashing winds,
Blew over my mantle,
Breaking to pieces,
My porcelain figurine.
(The wind was mean)

Shattering glass,
Pouring drops,
And the dashing winds
Were all fragments of my
Shattered dreams.

After even a longer pause, Dr.
Neiderbach then asked, "Wow Billy,
what does that mean?" For a moment, I

didn't know what she was referring to. With bewilderment in my eyes, she just rephrased her question, "How does the poem that you read tie into what you were feeling?" "Oh, that's what you meant. Well, after giving of myself for such a long time helping people, I guess I just didn't feel appreciated. It seemed as if all of my dreams were just washing away. It was like Mr. Clark or someone was trying to shatter them. All of my life, I gave to others. Helping was like freedom to me. It's like I see the birds when they're flying peacefully above all of the chaos that we experience daily. The wind is sooo calm and peaceful, but that same wind can enter my room and blow over my porcelain figurine.

Dr. Neiderbach just watched my lips as I spoke. I didn't know if she understood what I was saying, but I was just happy to know that she wanted to hear what I was feeling. I started to tell her more but I couldn't muster the energy to go back to that day of emptiness. So I waited for her to lead. She replied, "Wow, very interesting. Well Billy, continue what you were saying before I interrupted you."

It devastated me. "What are you referring to?" The fact that they decided to suspend me made me sad. So, as I was saying, I packed up all of my things and left. I felt everyone staring at me. My whole travel home I felt as though I was being followed. I looked back and saw what appeared to be the Devil chasing me, causing me to drop all of my belongings and dash for my home, where I remained for two months. I completely gave up on myself, and if couldn't save lives, what could I do? What is my purpose in life? If my life didn't have a purpose, is it worth living? I battled with this, as I would daydream on the edge of the roof tending to my babies. Then I decided my life wasn't worth living..."

Chapter 9
Fanatical Suspension

"Wait a minute, it seems like your rushing things." Dr. Neiderbach said. "What happened in those two months that caused for you to believe your life wasn't worth living?" She asked.

I just sat there with a blank look on my face. I've been in counseling with this beautiful white woman for many years and I still have never told her this part of my life. I guess I always wondered whether or not my story would be understood or simply measured and compared to everyone else's situation. For some reason, I got this strange feeling. It was as if there was something about that moment that told my soul, it was time; time for me to tell her the full story of what I experienced in those two months following. Maybe then will she completely understand me, or at least the man she sees in front of her.

"Bill-lllyyy ,"Dr. Neiderbach repeatedly called out until I became responsive. "Bill-lllyyy!" "Yes Shelly, I mean, Dr. Neiderbach" was my reply. I was paying attention the whole time that she was calling out my name. I just didn't really know if I should respond or not. She then repeated what she previously asked, "Tell me what happened two months following your suspension."

I stared at her with a dismissive look with almost a frustration in answering the question and said, "Suspension, if that's what you want to call it. I wasn't suspended, I just never got called back to work." It seemed as if she had no concern for what I had just told her. She just asked me the question again, "Can you just tell me what happened? You may not realize it, but we're seriously really running out of time."

I have never seen such a look of desperation in the eyes of Dr. Neiderbach, Shelly as I affectionately thought of her. I held to her request. "Well, after I was suspended and openly embarrassed in front of my peers, I walked out carrying a box of my belongings as everyone's eyes were fixed upon me. I passed by this one. He was wearing a blue pin-striped suit. It was strange that I would remember him, but the one thing most pronounced about his presence was that his shirt was buttoned all the way to the top. He wasn't wearing a tie around his collar. There was a woman who was also wearing a blue pants suit that accompanied him. I guess now when I think about it, their outfits were virtually identical.

As I walked out the office, I noticed that the two of them stopped at my superior's desk, who had just suspended me. It was then that I saw him point over in my direction. I was confused as to why he was pointing at me until I realized that those two people began running in my direction, so I ran. I didn't wait to see what they wanted or why they were chasing me. I just dropped everything that I was holding and took to flight. I rushed through the crowd knocking people over in the process. I apologized as I proceeded but never stopped to see if anyone was okay. I couldn't. I had to flee. I never even looked back until I got to the streets and noticed that there were no more people around me. I was completely surrounded by nothingness. Finally, I was alone. Within a split second of my solitude, they reappeared, right in my face; causing my heart to jump out of my chest.

'Are you Billy Michaels?' The woman asked. I paused for a moment to collect my thoughts. For some reason I thought about my brother Albie, maybe because I know if he was in my shoes he would have said no and came up with a clever story. Unfortunately, I was less imaginative in the lying department so I responded, 'Yes I am'. The man looked at me and spoke, 'We have a few questions for you about some of the cases that we are investigating in and out of the hospital and some fires that we've been working on.' 'Well, who the hell are you,' I asked. 'We're law enforcement officers from the Essex County Prosecutor's Office.' I paused for a moment before responding, 'Am I under arrest?' The man responded saying, 'No, not at all, we just want to ask you a few questions. 'Starting with? was my quick response. 'Exactly how many fires have you been the first person on scene?'

I just stood in silence; I would have never predicted that they would ask me such a question. And to know that the question that they were asking was part of their investigation, I would have never believed. I knew that silence was not a friend at this moment so I just answered, 'I'm not sure, maybe a few of 'em, I'm not really sure of the exact number.' The female officer seemed irritated by my response. That's when she leaped for me, grabbing me up by the collar and said, 'It's been nine houses damn houses that you torched and one of them…' The male officer then reached in to grab her arm and pulled her away from me. He appeared moved by her actions more than my answer to her question. As I saw, he began to counsel her in a whisper, to the point that I was unable to hear what they were talking about.

I was irritated by this act of disrespect; as I adjusted my shirt, back to order. Once I was able to gather myself from what I call an attack, I yelled out, 'What the hell you ask me for if ya'll already knew.' With no reply the man walked over leaving the woman to herself and said, 'Mr. Michaels, sorry for Detective Mitchells' actions. She was completely out of line. She's been under a lot of stress do to this investigation and of course, personal issues that she's been dealing with.' He stuck his hand out as if he wanted to shake hands. I ignored his advance to shake because it was with his left hand instead of his right. My Daddy always told me never to trust a man who would shake your hand with his left hand unless his right hand is missing. So I didn't even bother to shake it, rather I responded with, 'So, that's Detective Mitchells, who you?' He looked me square in the eye and replied, 'Detective Friday, now I have an additional question for you. Why is it that every patient under your care who was under life support, died?' 'Died, you mean…' I grabbed my chest as to the surprise that this man is implying that a patient whom I tended to died because of something I did.

That's when I knew the investigation was more in depth than I had originally assumed. I then murmured, 'I don't know.' Detective Mitchells must have heard me because she rushed back over to me with hate in her eyes, ready to attack me again, screaming, 'We know what you did, we know exactly what you did you sonofa….!' Luckily for me, Detective Friday interrupted her by placing his hand over her mouth as he held her back. Then he looked at me and said, 'We'll be in touch, make sure you don't leave the city.' I turned around to head back in the direction from which I ran and saw a crowd of people walking through the traffic. I then turned back to the detectives and they were gone. I have never been this confused and scared in my life.

The next thing I remembered was climbing up on my roof and finding myself disturbed by what I was witnessing. A group of alley cats had somehow broken into my Pigeon coop and were in process of slaughtering my children. So I rushed back down the ladder back to my room and grabbed a pillow case. I rushed back up to the roof tripping over each step and started grabbing these feisty felines who were even attempting to attack me. One by one I threw them into the pillow case. There were six in total. Once I collected them all, I twisted it to seal off the top and held it closed with my hand. I looked around to for survivors and they all were dead. Full of anger, I lost it and, and…"

"And, what Billy?" Dr. Neiderbach asked, "You're doing so well, please don't stop now."

There was a reason I stopped the story, but I knew that continuing to hold back information would only play to my disadvantage so with eyes full of tears and a mouth full of saliva, I proceeded with the story. "I had, I had the pillow case full of cats. It was right there in my hand. When I looked; I mean I saw all my children DEAD; just lying there, motionless, breathless they were, never to see another light of day again. This enraged me, so much so that my mind went blank. I had complete control of my actions, I think! To this day I still really don't know. All I can tell you is that, the site of blood and feathers simply outraged me and I began slamming the pillowcase against the rooftop repeatedly until I heard the painful screeching come to an agonized whisper.

I then left the roof and found myself in the alley near my house. There was a barrel that the homeless would gather around for warmth. I can still hear the cries from the cats echoing throughout the blood soaked pillowcase. So I then reached in my pocket for my trusty box of matches. I opened the box and to my surprise there was only two matches left inside. I grabbed one of the matches and struck it against the side of the matchbox. I dropped the lit match into the barrel and it was like instant combustion. It must have been soaked with booze or another fuel source. I stared at the flames for what seemed like hours and eventually... Eventually I just launched the pillow case into the fire. The screams! Oh my god the screams that those cats yelled out as they began the process of cremation haunted me for weeks. Sometimes when I close my eyes I can still here their squeals.

My world was seemingly falling apart. I lost my employment, my family and I was slowly losing my sense of well-being. I head to my front door and noticed a folded piece of paper sitting on the floor in front of my entrance. I picked up the paper and slowly unfolded it. Once opened it read, *We know what you did BILLY*. It wasn't written in no ones script, it was letters cut from a magazine. My first thought was that it was probably that angry female detective who for some reason had it out for me. So I just brushed it off and continued into my home. I placed the note on top of my side table, which contained all my miscellaneous mail, sat down on the couch and pulled my mother's hand-woven crochet blanket and covered myself to keep warm.

I woke up from what seemed like days later to a knocking at my front door. I get up to see who it was and a note is slid under the door. I then notice what appeared to be a shadow walking off. I ran to door to see who this mystery person was, but to no avail, there was no one there. I closed the door and walked over to the note. I opened it, unfolding its corners to reveal the letter's contents and I saw another magazine cut out letter which read, *Even when you're asleep, we're watching you. You will pay for what you did.*

This continued everyday for 46 days. There were times I couldn't even sleep because of fear that someone was watching me. It made my life a living hell. I could barely even leave my room. If it wasn't for the involuntary need to eat, I don't think I ever would have left. That is until the 47th day, when I was completely out of rations and needed to make a run to the market. Before I left the house for the first time in a month and a half I stopped to look at myself in the mirror. I found the site quite disturbing as I was still wearing my uniform from work. My face was filled with caked up dried skin and crud in the corners of my eyes. My hair looked nappy and dirty. It hadn't seen water or soap in weeks. I didn't care, even though I was accustomed to being net and clean.

I couldn't muster the energy to care how I looked. Normally I would have just groomed myself but I was not in the mood. I just left out with the sole intention to grab some food and return back to where I felt the safest. Once I exited my home, to my surprise there were the detectives just sitting there outside my door as if they had been waiting for me the whole time. 'Mr.

Michaels!' Detective Friday screamed out, as he and Detective Mitchell were beginning to stand and walk up to me. Out of fear I just ran back into the home. Once I slammed the door shut, they began banging on the opposite side so much that the door appeared to be coming off its hinges. I ran to the couch and grabbed for my phone. I dialed the first number that popped into my head and just began talking. That's when the banging stopped and another note was slid under my door. I slowly brought the phone down from ear and hesitantly approached the note. This one read, *It is time that you to paid for your sins. FIRE, DEATH, CATS! Your day of atonement draws near…* Not knowing what else to do I just placed the letter atop the others and headed for the bathroom. I needed to cleanse myself. I finally felt dirty.

Once in the bathroom I could hear the faint sounds of the phone off the hook but I ignored its cry and proceeded to run myself a bath hoping to cleanse myself of all impurities. My need to feed myself vanished. I looked to my left and noticed this purple candle, which was given to me as a gift from my mother to fight off evil spirits. I reached into my pocket and pulled out the last match from the box. I gazed at the candle for a moment and as I struck the match against the side of the box for the last time, I lit the candle and began to recite Psalm 29, a Psalm of David.

¹Give unto the LORD, O ye mighty, give unto the LORD glory and strength.

²Give unto the LORD the glory due unto his name; worship the LORD in the beauty of holiness.

³The voice of the LORD is upon the waters: the God of glory thundereth: the LORD is upon many waters.

That's when I noticed my bath water was nearly spilling over the tub. So I shut off the water and entered the tub. Continuing with the Psalm I recited, *⁷The voice of the LORD divideth the flames of fire.* While reciting, I just slowly closed my eyes and allowed myself to drift off. I opened my eyes only to see that I was completely surrounded by whiteness. 'Where was I?' was the only question in my mind. That's when I looked to the ground and saw all my family just lying on the floor motionless. For a second my heart wept, with the thought of the children I just lost. Then a noise that could only be compared to a flush occurred and water started to fill the room from the bottom of the walls to the ceiling. One by one the motionless birds began to move and started to float and fly away from the flooding waters. As the water rose to just below my chin, I looked around again and saw that I was all alone. So I just closed my eyes and fell into peace. I swallowed what was left of mommy's ibuprofen. I saw the way those drugs did her; so I figured that I too could fly away, fly high.

Drifting, drifting was the flight I took as I began to nod away from my reality. I saw myself asleep with the breeze of the ocean breathing on my face. It was as if my flight carried me to a distant shore. I….. "Bill-lllyyy, Bill-lllyyy, are you okay?" was the question posed by Dr. Neiderbach as I continued in fantasy and drift away. She continued, 'Is this something that you wrote about from before?' I responded, "Yeeeessss." Dr. Neiderbach said, 'So that I can truly understand you, can you just tell me what you wrote while you were feeling what you're feeling?" I began….

"A Star At Sea"

That yellow moon

Shining bright,

Sprayed its aura

Across a gleaming sea.

Its radiant light

That filled the sky,

Seemed to speak

Only at me.

Overwhelmed and ecstatic

Could barely describe,

Those sensations of romance

That exuberantly stole my heart.

Dressed by midnight,

With accessories made of draping stars,

The crested sea became her lap

As I laid waiting patiently.

Touching me softly

With her warm gentle breeze,

She fulfilled my dreams

Completely.

Filled with emotions

And tears in my eyes,

I know this feeling would only last

For two more hours.

So, not wanting to wait for her

To leave my sight,

I snuggled into a ball

With her at may side.

Thank you and Good Night, my Dear

For this evening we've shared,

I just hope to see you

The next time that I sail."

That's when those old familiar hands of my brother Albert grabbed me as I opened my eyes, pulling me out from the water. 'What in hell are you doing Billy, what are you trying to do?' He frantically screamed out as he wrestled to pull me to dry land. I never responded. I just stayed quiet, aside from the coughing and gasping for air.

Next thing I knew, he grabbed me with much force, plopping me onto the bathroom floor and dragging me to my couch. Albert said that when he pulled me from the water, he noticed an empty medicine bottle with my mom's name on it as he sat across from me, gasping for air as if he had just run a marathon. I looked down at myself and saw I was still wearing my same dirty work uniform. They were soaked and wet and I had a blanket around me. While trying to catch his breath he ask, 'Is everything ok with you? In the softest of voice and defeated by shame I replied, 'Yeah, Yeah, I'm okay!" for the life in me I couldn't figure it out for nothing in the world why he would be asking me that, there's no way everything is ok. I'm trying to kill myself. I just wanted all of this to go away. Albie said, 'It was a good thing you called me first and I was able to rush right over here. Now tell me what's going on with you. You haven't been yourself lately. Mommy was concerned about you as well. She will be here in a minute.' I just pointed to the pile of papers that were on the table near the door. He followed my finger to see where I was pointing and walked over to the table. He then pointed to the papers and said, 'These?' I shook my head yes as he picked them up and brought them back over to where I was sitting.

'These are just flyers and take out menus. What do you need with them?' He asked. I then stood up out my seat with all the energy that I could muster and began stumbling backwards as I snatched the papers from out of my brothers' hand. He was right! They were just flyers, menus and coupons. I could only think about what happened to those letters someone was leaving behind I thought to myself, but I stayed silent. 'Billy, say something! What's going on with you bro?!' Albert asked.

So I finally spoke, with tears flooding my eyes, 'Man, I'm in so much trouble. I got suspended from work, they started an investigation and now they have these detectives following me everywhere I go. I don't know what else to do.' Albert just looked at me with an oddly confused look then said, 'What are you talking about? I just spoke with your job. Right after you called me rambling, I called you right back thinking you were at the hospital but they said you haven't been to work in over two weeks. There was no mention of an investigation; just that you haven't showed up to work and they were surprised because you were just promoted, so I rushed right over.' I thought I was confused before but after hearing those words from my brother, all I could think was, *This can't be true, what have I been doing all this time? And if it is true, what's wrong with me?* So I just sat muted, my mouth moved but no words escaped, until… Until…"

"Until, what Billy? Did your mom ever show up?" Dr. Neiderbach asked.

Chapter 10
Mom's Mouth to Doc's Ears

Mommy showed up, but as soon as she walked in, she wasn't alone." I replied. "What do you mean she wasn't alone?" asked Dr. Neiderbach. So I explained, "When my mom came to my home she was accompanied by the two detectives. With a face of confusion, Dr. Neiderbach continued to listen. So I continued….. Well, the site of them caused for me to jump out of my chair screaming, 'There they go, there they go! Mommy, watch out for them. They're behind you!' It was then that my brother Albert turned around with disappointment in his eyes and said, 'What's wrong with you boy, that's your momma,' he said. I looked back over to where mommy was standing and could still see the detectives taunting me. It was then that I asked, 'Mommy, do you see that man and woman standing next to you?' She didn't answer, rather she just broke out into tears crying, 'Oh God, Billy! My baby! Lord, what done happen to my Billy, what's wrong with my baby?' She cried out. Full of sadness and concern she cautiously approached and reached towards me to give me a big hug. 'Come here Baby, it's gon be ok, don't worry, Momma's here, everything's gonna be alright,' as she whispered while hugging me.

I didn't know what to do at this point. I started realizing that everything that I had thought to be real for the past two months really wasn't. I'm seeing people no one else can see and finding out that instead of two months, it's only been two weeks. *Is it me or am I just going crazy,* was my only thought. ' I've always heard that if you think you're the only one feeling a certain way then maybe it is true that you might be the one with the issue.

My mom pulled back from our hug and said, 'Wow Billy! You're soaking wet?' I didn't respond. I just stayed silent. Albert, on the other hand, was more than willing to speak out for me. 'He tried to baptize himself in his bathtub! 'What!,' momma yelped. Albert continued, 'Luckily I got here when I did or he'd be dead in his heaven right about now!' After mommy's initial response, silence engulfed the room for fear of what was to come. 'Is this true Billy? Did you, did you try to take your own life?' She asked me. I couldn't speak a word, because the detectives were standing there behind her motioning me to keep my mouth shut. I believe my silence frustrated her because she started to shake me, somewhat violently yelling, 'Billy, answer me boy! What's wrong with you?'

There was something about that outburst that somehow snapped me out of the comatose state that I was in. For the first time since my Mom walked in, I was able to look her in the eyes and gather my thoughts. I finally responded, 'I don't know, I don't know mommy. I think I need help.' Albert butted in, 'You right you need some help, trying to take your own life. How selfish is that?' 'Quiet Albert!' Mommy said, 'Be kind to your brutha. Something is obviously wrong and we need to get him some professional help. Why don't you just head on back home, I can take it from here!' Albert didn't say anything; rather he just walked over to Mom and gave her a kiss on the forehead before he exited.

At the time I had no idea why my Mom wanted to speak to me alone, but the look on her face let me know that the conversation was going to be serious. Once Albert closed the door behind him, my Mom walked over and grabbed my phone and began to dial a number. I later found out it was you. She started talking saying, 'Hi, this is Mrs. Michaels, may I speak to Dr. Neiderbach please? Tell her Josephine.....Ok, I'll hold... (a long pause) Hey Shelly, it's me, Mrs. Micheals... I could be better... Well, it's an emergency......My son needs you......Well, I'd rather you and him have that discussion cause it seems as if he's in another one of those crisis moods......Yes.....Are you free today? Well....In one hour? That'll be perfect. Thank you so much, we'll see you soon.' Then she hung up the phone and walked back over to me. I asked, 'Who needs who?' was my question to my mother. She replied by saying, 'It's Neiderbach, don't you remember her? She's your former childhood therapist. "Therapist," was my only response. She's a Clinical Forensic Psychologist and even if you don't remember her, it would be beneficial to speak with her anyway. We'll be meeting her in a bit.' 'Forensic Psychiatrist?' I asked again, 'What do I need to speak to her about? They're for crazy people.' She looked at me with a look of surprise and concern and said, 'Son, don't worry yourself if you don't remember Dr. Neiderbach? No son. She's just someone for you to speak with about what you've been going through. She helps people by teaching them how to deal with different types situations. It's not fair to label her as one who sees crazy people. And for the record, you're not crazy.'

I just looked away from my mother, she must have really believed I was going crazy or something. The fact of the matter is, I had no idea what was happening to me. I could still see the detectives periodically going in and out while they listened to our conversation. For the life in me, I could only wonder why they never said anything to make themselves known. Maybe they were in some type of cloak that only I could see. My mind just kept wondering that maybe they're gathering Intel on me. Maybe they just wanted to make me look crazy. Either way my Mom was convinced that her baby boy needed some psychiatric help.

'Mommy, do you think I'm crazy?' I asked my mother. She just stood up and said, 'I honestly don't know what to think. That's why I called the doctor so you can speak with her and she can give you a proper answer. I'm just worried about you. You tried to take your own life... You have any idea how much that hurts me?' I have witnessed my mother go through a rollercoaster of emotions in my lifetime but the expressions she was displaying at that moment was a whole other animal, one that my weak emotions couldn't tame at the moment.

So I joined her in her cry as I apologized, 'I'm sorry Momma, I'm sorry. I never wanted you to hurt. I'm sorry. I feel a little strange, somewhat weird. I sometime feel scared for no reason. I see people who aren't there and I even hear voices speaking to me. I just don't know what I'm going through or how to deal with it. It's just been so much pain lately, I just wanted to fly freely, fly high and away.' Mommy was quiet until my last statement and simply asked, 'Why do you want to fly away son?' I paused for a moment and said, 'it seems as if life has clipped my wings. I just don't know another way to be free.' I could look at her eyes and see the same judgment that others who didn't know or understand me have shown and it made me sick to my stomach. How could my own mother be looking at me like this, as if I'm some type of stranger or just merely crazy.

She spoke again saying, 'The part that hurts me the most is that you tried to take your own life. Son, good, bad, or indifferent, this is the life that I gave you. You have any idea how selfish it is to wanna take your life? I know I told you of my experiences while giving birth to you and how the doctors later told me that my heart flat-lined. Never once did I explain to you what preceded that miracle. When I was in labor the doctor explained to me and your father that you had Amniotic Fluid Embolism which is a rare and incompletely understood obstetric emergency in which amniotic fluid, fetal cells, hair, and other debris entered my bloodstream through the placenta bed of my uterus causing an allergic reaction that lead to me having cardio-respiratory failure. To complicate matters even more, the umbilical cord was wrapped around your neck choking you to death; I had already lost too much blood.

The doctor warned us that proceeding with the delivery could cause for me to lose my life and even possibly yours. The doctor's suggested to us that it may be best to terminate the pregnancy in order to spare of my own. It was then that I made the decision that it wasn't something that I could do. So I told the doctor to continue with the delivery because no matter what, I wanted your life to have a chance. It's only by the Grace of God that we both survived and my sacrifice wasn't in vain and my feelings are the same even today. I don't regret my decision. So you see, by attempting to take your own life, you were also killing a part of me. Since the day of your birth we have been eternally connected and we've shared a bond that's unbreakable. I just need for you to cherish the gift of life you possess and never again take it for granted.'

When my mother told me that; I was at a lost for words. I looked over to the detectives and Detective Mitchells in an arrogant voice asked, 'If your Mommy was willing to give up her life for you, that means she doesn't value her own. So why should you?' That question really struck a nerve as I yelled out, 'Shut up, shut up.... leave me alone,' while grabbing my head and spiraling down to the ground. I was speaking to the detectives who were standing behind my mom but it appeared as if she assumed I was speaking to her. She countered with, 'Billy, who....Who the HELL do you think you talking to boy?' I was shocked, I never heard my Mom speak in such a manner before, so I quick tried to remedy the situation by apologizing, 'I'm sorry Mommy. I wasn't speaking to you. I was talking to them.' 'What?' She asked. 'I was talking to.......'

That's when I decided that if I was in a room with someone that only spoke to me and no one else acknowledged them. I wouldn't openly acknowledge them either. The last thing I want to do is be judged and considered crazy. As a result I turned to my Mother and answered with, 'Never mind! I don't know what I'm saying anymore. I think I need to just get some rest; I haven't really had a chance to get much sleep lately. That could be the cause for my so called delusional state.' Looking at my mother I could tell that this excuse didn't fly as she simply said, 'I think we need a second opinion so go change into some dry clothes and let's get ready to head over to meet Dr. Neiderbach. She opened up her schedule just to meet with us. I don't want to be late.'

There was no need for me to even put up a fight, so I just got up and walked to my bedroom with my head down in shame and disappointment. I entered the bedroom and began to undress. I put on some dry clothes and met mommy back in the living room. She was sitting with the detectives. She appeared oblivious as to their presence around her. When I walked in all three of them looked at me, but I only acknowledged my mother by saying, 'Are you ready to go?' She rose off the sofa and we exited my home."

Dr. Neiderbach interrupts, "Yes, that wasn't the first time that we met. We first met when you were a little boy when your parents sent you to stay with me and my other friends at the camp in the hills. You were sooo young at the time. However, I do remember that time when you came into my office. You had barely turned 20 and were troubled with problems of someone three times your age." I smiled at Dr. Neiderbach and said, "I remember meeting you too, your fro was so high and elegant. You were the first white woman that I had ever seen with an afro. I didn't know if you were a light-skinned black woman or just somebody with a blowout. In any case, you relaxed me so I felt you were able to relate to my pains. That made it easier for me to talk to you." She responded with a disappointed look and said, 'If that's true Billy, why has it taken you so long to tell me about the fact that you were seeing people over 30 years ago? Has it continued since our first session."

I didn't know how to answer that question because there were times I couldn't tell if the person in front of me was actually there or if it was just an illusion created by the thoughts. I studied her questions in my mind before answering then I looked up at her and saw Detective Mitchells standing by the window, so I answered her, "Sometimes, but I can hardly tell anymore." Dr. Neiderbach looked at me with a look of relief once I said that, as if I had answered the question she was looking for or I provided the puzzle piece she has been missing. Then she said, "We have really made progress with these series of talks. I think I found a way I could help you with your trial tomorrow. From the information I gathered over this past week, I believe with Jerry's help we can get your sentence reduced from first degree murder to a lesser sentence due to mitigating circumstances."

"Murder? Murder who? Who murdered who Doc? They think I...?" I asked in an outraged tone. A guard walked in and Dr. Neiderbach waved him to leave then said, "Calm down Billy, calm down. When you were arrested they told you what you were being convicted of…., but I see that because we are running short on time, I can't rely on your memory. You were charged with the murder of your…"

Dr. Neiderbach was interrupted again by the guard who says, "Sorry to disturb your session but your time has drawn to an end. The prisoner has to face trial in the morning and I was ordered to relieve you of your duties. I can give you two more minutes to wrap up, but that's it." "Okay, thank you officer" was her reply. Then she turned to me and said, "You need to get your rest Bill-lllyyy. I want you to know you did great and I'll be with you tomorrow in full support of your well-being." She started packing up her things and began to head for the door. "Wait!" I yelled out, "Who was murdered?" For a moment, she paused. Obviously wanting to say something, she just looked at me with a saddened look and said, "It was your…" before she could finish her thought the door opened up again with the same guard saying, "It's time." Dr. Neiderbach turned to me and said, "I have to go, I'll see you in the morning. Don't forget to write if you find yourself getting frustrated. Just remember to write and believe only 10% of what you see."

As she vanished from my view, I was left by myself to ponder on all of my fears. I began to search my surroundings only to find comfort in staring at the ceiling. With tears running down my cheeks I began to hum this old gospel tune that my mother to rock me to sleep. It went,

'My mother was, so good and kind
She often told me, son you're mine
As she sang, her song that day
Amazing Grace……'

Momma meant everything to me. I miss her presence because she had a never-ending way of soothing my fears, no matter how old I got.

Chapter 11
Freedom

In the background it softly played.....

'I need thee
Oh I need thee
Every hour, I need thee
Oh bless me now my savior
I come to thee
I need thee oh, I need thee
Every hour, I need thee.....'

Shhhh!! Shhhh! (with the softest whisper) It's just me. I know. I know. It's not going to hurt. Shhhh! Please, please don't cry. Awe, no! I'm sorry! I just wanna help you, was my plea as I took my left hand and gently placed it on her forehead, softly stroking her to sleep. I began to sing, 'I need thee.' I don't know if it was for me or her, I just felt it in my spirit. As this saint goes on to glory, I kept on singing. 'I need, thee oh, I......'

'Hey, hey you, it's time for us to take you back to your cell,' was the order of the guards as they awoke me from my dream. I was startled by their assertiveness and lack of sensitivity. They had to have known by just looking at me that I was well asleep in my own world. I don't know where my dream was taking me. All that I do know is that I'm feeling a sensation that I had never experienced before, one of total freedom. It's a feeling that makes me sing, 'I need, thee oh, I need thee. For some odd reasons, my emotions are beginning to get the best of me. I'm starting to tear. If it wasn't for the cuffs around my wrists, I would wipe them away. I wouldn't want them to see me weak in any way.

I laid quietly as they gathered around my bedside. I couldn't hear what all that they were discussing, so I just observed whatever I could until… I saw a lady in a white medical robe approach the guards. I could only wonder why she was present. I tried to hear what they were discussing. As she got closer to where I laid, I asked her, 'ma'am, what's going on?' She kindly looked at me with the most pleasant of expressions and just smiled. She never responded to my question. She began to inject a clear liquid in this I.V. line that was attached to the bottom of the saline bottle. I felt so offended that she too ignored me. It seemed as if no one was willing to give me any direct attention or answers until I.........

'With all of the strength that I could muster, I forced myself up from the gurney in outrage as to why no one is giving me any answers to what is going on in my life. I tried to grab her hand as she reached over me to inject the sedative in the saline bag, but due to my restrictions my hands were limited. As I lunged in her direction, I was able to grab with my teeth, the inner part of her bicep, forcing her to yelp in pain from the hold of my bite. 'What are you doing to me' was my forced question from between my teeth. No sooner than she yelped, I could see the guards running towards me. One of them used his billyclub to smash me up beside my forehead while the other grabbed me around my throat yelling at me to release her from my grip. At that moment, I didn't care what pain they were attempting to cause me. I just needed them to know that I'm not a guinea pig and I needed answers.

The power of the guard's grip around my neck forced me to release my bite from her arm. As the nurse pulled back wincing from the pain that I caused her, I could hear amongst the commotion, the guards asking her if she was able to give me the medication. As I turned to see the label of the medication, it seemed as if everything around began moving in slow motion. I knew they had given me something strong to sedate me but I for once felt victorious because I wasn't going to let them take me down without a fight.

I'm beginning to feel the burning

sensation of the medication running through my arms, down the front of my legs and up through my buttocks, around my back and finally igniting in my chest. It's like a fire being ignited by a match stick; the closer it gets to your fingers the hotter the temperature. I slowly feel myself falling back on the gurney as the lights and ceiling begins to spin. As my head slope over my right shoulder, I could feel the drool rolling down from the corner of my mouth, rolling over my cheek.

As they began to push me through the hall, the lights above me began to lull me into a false sense of security, making me believe that it's alright to put my guard down. The motion of the stretcher racing through the prison hallways with the lights to shade made me nauseous to the point I began vomiting all the way back to my cell. With no concern for my well-being, I could hear the guards saying throw that motherfucker in his cave. Powerless from the sedative and at their mercy, I was thrown to the floor to fetch for myself as I laid in my own vomit and excrement.

'Lights out' was the yell that shortly followed their exit from my cell. My rage began to get the best of me. I wanted to grab, stab, beat, destroy all who came within reach of me. I tried my best to get up only to fall back to the ground. Even with the sedative, I was still conscious enough to know where I was. I was determined not to give up. For the next hour or so, I was able to pull myself up onto my familiar bed. This bed of which mattress I despised has now become the haven of my comfort, at least for the remainder of that evening.

Drip, drip, drip, drip…… I began to count each drip to each second hoping that my time will quickly pass away. After 10 minutes of that nonsense, I got exhausted from the fatigue of earlier today that I started feeling lighter and lighter, as if I was beginning to fly, fly, fly far away.

'Who's there' was my cry as the room got darker and darker. Albie, Antney, where are you? Are you guys home? Antney was staying with momma for the past year or so. He too suffered from that debilitating ailment of arrested development, not living life on its terms. I'm almost certain that if he would just take the time to look at himself and be honest with making adjustments to change, he will eradicate all lingering symptoms of his disease. I always hope that he would help momma a little more than he did but, life goes on.

I waited before moving through the doorway, ensuring that I was alone with my thoughts. Everyone seemed to hold vigils of mommy at her bedside, while she laid sedated with every pain medication that one could imagine. I needed her more now in my life than ever before. I needed her to feel me and know that I'm here for her just as when she was there for me. There it goes again, the sounds of that old gospel music that she loved to play on Sunday mornings, 'I need thee Oh, I need thee. Every hour, I...... Mommy, I'm home.

While slowly passing through her front room, I couldn't help but observe what appeared to be old crochet cloths that she must have been working on for someone prior to her falling ill. My mind took me back to the day when I was sick with the flu. She wrapped me in this colorful blanket. I must have been bout nine or so. That same pattern appeared to be the design of the cloth that I was holding in my hand. With me now coming to her rescue, I began to tear from the thoughts of how she cradled me that long dark day. Maybe this is the one she's making for herself, considering the circumstances.

The roaring sounds of the wind and thunderous sounds of the lightning are scaring me and causing me to question my very existence. Through the bent blinds, a ray of light peaks, illuminating objects and pictures that have found their havens in the depths of mommy's cave. Just to the right of where her chair rested on the wall, I noticed the collage of pictures that decorated the living room wall of my father and grandmother who have since gone on. I could only wonder why those very pictures that I adored have now come to haunt me. It's as if they're now staring at me with a purpose. Am I wrong?

Amongst the photos I see this little boy holding his pigeon. Is that me? The closer I got to the wall, the more nervous I got. I remember that day as if it was yesterday. It had to have been one of the saddest days of my life. On the rooftop these stray cats broke into my pigeon coop and killed most to all of my pets. It wasn't until the next day that I realized that my friend Ralphie was able to survive the attack. Somehow, by the time I was able to rescue Ralphie, he made it over to my next door neighbor's roof in his attempt to flee the carnage. Ralphie was the leader of the bunch. Even though he was no more than my pet bird, he was there for me every time I needed company. He was my best friend. To see that Ralphie wasn't dead, brought me joy and anger. I tried in every possible way to treat him of his wounds, but he was still losing too much blood and his fight for his life. It was then that Cousin Trent took that picture of me holding my best friend in my hands. That day I'll never forget it.

As I proceed into the next room, I noticed the electric piano on the wall, the source for the music that kept Mommy company. That was a gift to mommy from daddy when he got caught fooling around with his mistress. For some odd reason I began to humm,

"Sweep over my soul, sweep ov'r my soul. Sweet spirit, sweep ov'r my soul. My life is complete, as I knell at his feet. Oh sweet spirit, sweep ov'r……..

As I rustled through the cards that rested on the end table, all of which are get well wishes. People with their selfish needs, had hopes for mommy to get better. In as much as I can understand the human agony of watching a loved one suffer, I am more persuaded to free them of their pain. I remember when my dad was on his deathbed after the fire, with all of his physical pains from the burns, he was still refusing to take any pain medication. Thank God Trent didn't suffer. However, when Daddy was asked to get better so that he could return home, his response was simple, 'for what?' I'm glad I was there for him then, just as today I am for mommy.

No sooner than I looked over my right shoulder, I screamed. Once again I'm startled at the image in the mirror. It's mommy lying asleep in her own bed with this monster of a machine breathing for her. It's huffing and puffing to raise her lungs to pass air through her body. It's a struggle to see her this way. As I glanced away, I still heard the machines. I wanted to go over and comfort her to ease her of her pain, but I soon realized that there were no machines. She was just off to sleep. I wanted to go in there and comfort her, letting her know that I was by her side, but I kept pulling away from her for fear of what I might be capable of doing.

I began breathing uncontrollably heavy; my anxieties are getting the best of me. I'm feeling as if I'm losing all control of my ability to think logically. I want with all that is in me to free mommy of her suffering. I hate seeing her in this way. I must end her agony now. 'Mommy, Mommy' was my whisper as I began walking towards her bedroom door.

"Tap, Tap, Tap" was the noise that startled me. As I quickly turned around to see from where the noise was originating, a bright beam of light blurred my vision. 'Keep it down,' was the order of the guard as he beat his baton on the cell bars. I quickly raised my hand to block the blinding beam from scorching my sight. As I squinted through the crack between my fingers, I saw that same nurse and the two guards who brought me this cell. Why are they torturing me was the inquiry that I could only ask myself. I wanted more than ever to escape from this pissy ass rathole.

'What do you want now' was my question to the trio. I could hear them saying something, but for the life in me, I couldn't figure out what they were discussing. "What time is it" was my only question. A quick response from one of the guards followed, "it's 3am." I could also hear the other guard saying,

'I hope he gets the gas chamber.' Before I could utter a word and just as quickly as they came in, they disappeared to leave me to my thoughts.

Every time that I thought of brutality and harsh treatment to others, I can't help but think about Daddy and his experiences during the Civil rights Movement. This is where my mind keep taking me every time that I see these jokers. It's as if my hatred for those who abuse authority increase. Had I my freedom, I would show them just how strong and mighty I truly am.

I turned back to my thoughts as I adjusted myself on the mattress. While seeking comfort as I laid, I felt something poke me from under the mattress. To my surprise, it was that same hidden pencil and pad that Dr. Neiderback gave me before she left. It was then that I just reached for it and began writing all of what I was feeling. In spite this incarceration; I still feel a sense of freedom because no chains, bars, shackles, or man is going to take my freedom away from me. I began writing about daddy's stories. To me, in spite my anger with him, he was the ultimate African American Man. If he was in my shoes, he'd tell these jokers about respecting who he is as a man. It was then that I wrote:

The African American Negro Man

Ship smelling hollows
Cold damp weather,
Wearing down my body
As I powered the vessel from below.

Sea water splashing in my face,
Through the holes made by the sea stones,
As the ship sped at a constant pace.

Chango, Chango to my God I cried
As each whip lashed across my back.
Please take me away from these friends I found,
Who has convinced my brothers with his lies.

He invaded my mother and stole from my sisters
So that I could see his fulfillment, What a perverse
task.
A poking heart and burning soul
I felt as if he raped me.

I was sold on the corners of Chestnut and Vine
Chained to an iron block.
I had to appear mighty and strong
Knowing these injustices were crimes.

While plowing the land I spoke with my brothers
About our great escape,
Designed by my mother, Ms Harriet
Signing a song about a plan.

Crowded streets and zoot suits became my living
style
I straightened my hair to look like them
Changing my identity from the south
As I rode the bus to Uncle Charles
Behind Aunt Rosa for a while.

Water flowing from the same streams
Drainage pipes depositing into the same sewage
pans
So sitting at their counters and drinking from their
faucets became a dream.

So today I sit and tell everyone
Of this story of me.
The African American Negro Man,
Sincerely!

For the remainder of the evening, I
wrote and wrote until day break.

Chapter 12

Peaceful Trail of Uncertainty

This was the first time in a while that I woke up by myself. No detectives, no Dr. Neiderbach, just me alone with my thoughts. This may have been a gift from God or just a curse, because all I could think about was my pending trial which was only moments away. I began to think about the people in my life who I may have wanted to help and also about the people I would never wanted to lose. At first thought, maybe it was my father and Trent's deaths that were brought upon at my hands or maybe one of my siblings was the cause of that. I really feel bad for what happen to Trent but, with all the physical and psychological torture my dad put me through life has a way of justifying its wrongs. The only good thing is that he passed off so much knowledge and bestowed so much of himself and sacrificed for our family. I really didn't want to lose him either, but some things are out of my control. Right now I could only wish that I had more time with my friend, Dr. Neiderbach. Then maybe I would have had some questions answered.

The sound of the door opening causes me to adjust myself in the bed. I look over at the door and there is two guards standing there. The one guard who was here with Dr. Neiderbach and I said, "Mr. Billy Ray Michaels, your trial awaits." He walked over to the bed and un-cuffed the handcuff attached to the bed rail and allowed me to sit up. He then took that cuff and placed it tightly around my free wrist. That's when the other guard entered and applied shackles to my feet. They lifted me to my feet and said, "Come with us please Mr. Michaels."

I was surprised by the pleasant tone of the guard as he spoke with. It was seemingly like I had a choice in the matter. Then I looked down at my metallic restrictions and realized that it was just a courtesy. They walked me out of the room, but because of the chains around my ankles I could only take small steps.

We got to the hallway and it was almost complete darkness. There were cones of light overhead but they were spaced out about six feet apart so in between the lights were totally shaded. This is it, was my thought to myself, 'time for me to find out why I was on trial; why I'm being referred to as the family man and besides, hear slurry comments seeping in of murder.' However strange, parts of me were excited while the rest of me was totally in fear. I had no idea what would await me at the end of this long walk but I continued it nonetheless.

The guards didn't speak a word, just walked silently as if they also knew that this was the end for me. Though I was confined; when we would pass through the darkness, I felt at peace. Maybe it was the silence that I found so pleasant or the sporadic darkness that relaxed me so. I don't know, but I felt at peace for once.

My baby steps just lead me into the light now where I see clearly and my mind wonders to moments of my childhood; all the times my brothers, sisters and I would have fun simply by being with each other. When we would sit around the table with Mommy's great cooking while Daddy told us stories of his past. The secrets we shared with other, games we played, how I learned friendship through family, and the most important of things, what I learned about myself. I began remembering those moments of happiness...

Then like a flash I was back into the shadows. Now all I can think about is the harm my father would bring with his creative ways of discipline; that he chose to demonstrate on my siblings and I. The many times he clipped my wings and whipped the feathers off my behind. How I watched him torment my brothers and regulate my sisters. The times when all I knew was pain…

My emotions switch just as the illumination I stepped into. I'm now thinking of my cousin Trent. Reminiscing on the times we shared. The mischief we would get into with my brother Albie. How sad I was to find out he was trapped in the bathroom the night of the fire, but relieved that he was now free to soar amongst the heavens. The happiness the fire brought me by freeing me from that ghetto of a place and allowing me to relocate somewhere else, anywhere. Even the denial of the insurance claim and the pending lawsuit brought to my family that was denied at our time of need. It forced us to finally be a family again, close, at least that's what I thought. Times when I was at ease…

I step back into darkness and the shallow depths of my subconscious takes over and I think of all my resentments; resentment towards my mother for her turning her back while we were attacked by my father: physically, verbally and emotionally. How she sacrificed her life for mine, then threw it in my face. The times when I really needed her, she was never there. My moments of bitterness...

Much as a slinky, my curved mind straightened at my next step. Under the fluorescence I recall my first love, Elise & my mission. My goal was to help families in need and teach them that through pain and loss; fortune and happiness can grow. I can't imagine the exact number of families I've helped and lives I've changed, to say over 50 would be an understatement to say over 100 would just be bragging. Just knowing I was able to have such a powerful impact on so many people would always brighten my day, until...

Again I'm surrounded by gloom. I feel

my left foot cut in front of my right causing gusts of wind to swim around my body. It's like I'm flying so I close my eyes to enjoy the soar. I take a quick peek to view my destination and all I could see was a shadowed ground quickly approaching. Now I fall alone, forced to face life's gravel on my own, I guess I'll just shut my eyes, it's always safe here.

I find myself lost in a recurring dream that I used to have as a small child, usually I would start off in my bedroom; this time, for the first time; I began the dream by falling off my Griffin. The pain soaring throughout my body is excruciating. I'm forced to fight through the agony just to stand up, but I can't. The only motion I have is in my neck as I start to look around. Surrounded by fiery disaster and destruction I hear a woman's voice calling my name. "Billy! Billy, No!" I look around to see where it was coming from then a window caught my eye.

Inside of the window I watched myself as a young adult exiting the bedroom of my first home. Outside of the window was inflamed but the interior played like a movie. I see myself stopping next to the couch and my mother is sitting there. I believe this was the moment before I met the psychiatrist for the first time because next to my mother sat Detectives Mitchell and Friday. I always remembered just walking out with my mother then meeting Dr. Neiderbach but this time was a lot different. Detective Mitchell walks over to the "Me" in the window and whispers something in his ear, then she stepped back with an evil smile upon her face. Whatever she said to him, caused for him to go into an outrage; because I watched myself start to slam everything in sight. The "Me" through the window was picking up everything and anything, while Mom just sat there with terror in her eyes watching his every moment.

After pile driving the side table into the floor, Detective Friday walks over and hands

*the "Me" through the window one of the
legs which broke off the table, whispers
something in his ear, then stepped back with
an evil smile upon his face right beside
Detective Mitchell. For a few seconds I
watched myself just stand there with a blank
look holding the table leg in our left hand.
Then as quick as the flap of an eagle's wing,
he raised the table leg over head and began
to rush mother. That must have been the
screaming as I heard, "Billy, Billy, No!"
Echoing throughout the darkness...*

*I shut my eyes so I could no longer see the
man through the looking glass for fear of
what he may have been doing. The
screaming has stopped but it's followed by
the screeching of what sounds like a police
siren. I close my eyes tighter and feel my
Griffin come for me and lift me from the
earth. The wind feels so good against my
skin. I hear someone calling my name "Billy,
Billy, are you ok?" So I open my eyes to see
who my savior is.*

To my surprise I open my eyes and see

the same old sweaty man in the suit I was with before he looks both upset and nervous as he helps get me off the floor and put me into my seat. "Counsel, please advise the defendant that if he can't stay awake in my courtroom, I'll just hold him in contempt and continue the case without him." The judge said. The sweaty old man just replied, "Yes your honor." I composed myself in my seat and leaned over to speak to the guy I am now assuming is my lawyer and I asked, "What happened?" He looked at me with a disappointed look that I knew all too well and whispered, "You keep falling asleep, then you fell out of your chair. The Jury just came back with their decision." "Was Dr. Neiderbach able to bring you the information she said she had to help my case?" I asked him. He looked at me even more confused than before then asked, "Who's Dr. Neiderbach?"

I was completely lost and confused at this point I had no idea what to do so I just let my eyes wander. Looking around everyone is standing except the person who was drawing the picture, the lady typing and me. "Counsel please inform the defendant that he's not excluded from rising with everyone else." The judge says in an irritated voice which causes my lawyer to nudge me to stand and I do so very versus William Ray Michaels; how do you the Jury find the defendant." An older black man wearing a Cosby sweater and glasses seems to be answering for everyone, "In the case of First Degree Murder for Mrs. JP Michaels; we the jury find the defendant, NOT GUILTY by reason of Insanity!"

TO BE CONTINUED...

November 10, 1994
5:15 PM

America Redefined

I offer to you a proposition that we collectively put an end to the stereotypes that deplete the characters of my fellow friends.

We must mute the sirens that play to the tunes of racism, separatism, inequality, and prejudice. It is not fair that society continues to hide behind a blanket of racism that has been inspired by fear and ignorance.

Racism, along with its counterparts – classism, sexism, ageism, etc. feed into the concept of separatism. It is not justifiable to simply say, "I'm Sorry" when you have deliberately and wrongfully accused another for a crime in which you have committed. Conversely, neither is it fair for me to accuse a community for the act of an individual.

For this, there is a need to institute a proposition that counters the drive towards separatism from any source; inequality towards a group; or racism against a people. One's color does not designate the directions of one's goals, the extent of one's intelligence, or the quality of one's character.

This proposition must first in its pledge, redefine what the American Dream is about. We must implement a new strategy that highlights education as the major

269

factor in defeating ignorance. Unless and until we address the uselessness of the ideas supporting racism, sexism, classism, etc., ignorance will eventuate this driving force of oppression for all people.

Sincerely,

William Michael Barbee

This letter is the response to the recent killings of two South Carolinian children by their mother.

EPILOGUE

After serving four years at The Greystone
Mental Hospital on related charges, Billy
Ray Michaels is released into a halfway
house somewhere in Newark, NJ. Billy
struggled long to maintain his sanity while
trying to acclimate to society. He sought the
support of his family, only to find that they
were divided in their support for him. Billy
Ray's brothers, Antney and Albie continued
on with their lives, committed to never
speak with their youngest brother again. For
his first year of being institutionalized, his
sister Martha made routine visits to see him
until her health became compromised by her
asthma. His older sister Jeannawillis ended
her visits just over the last year of him
serving out his sentence, due to the
relocation of her and her husband, Bobby, to
the south.

While in recovery, Billy Ray is ordered to
attend an outpatient psychiatric center where
he meets his new court appointed
psychologist, Dr. William Howard M.
Griffith. Dr. Griffith revealed to Billy that
his former childhood psychotherapist, Dr.
Shelly Neiderbach called and is inquiring

about his well being. According to Griffith, while in his 3rd month of sessions with Billie, he began having hallucinations as to the type of relationship he shared with Dr. Neiderbach. Griffith said during a phone conversation with Neiderbach, *"while Billie was in a hypnotic state of consciousness, he began moaning and calling out your name as if he was making love to you. It was strange to hear and see him gyrating as if you were on top of him."* Quietness engulfs the conversation, causing Griffith to push for more information. Neiderbach declined to go any further in the conversation, only saying that they needed to talk in person rather than over the phone.

Billy finally completes his required counseling sessions with Dr. Griffith. He gets hired at the halfway house as a counselor, in which he once was a client. Upon helping others with their issues, Billy finds himself once again entangled in his own web of confusion and deceit.

ABOUT THE AUTHOR

WILLIAM MICHAEL BARBEE, is an entrepreneur and artist who believes that all of God's creations are beautiful. Over the past 15 years, he's been able to merge his expertise in business with his innate artistic abilities by developing multiple businesses while staying true to his creativity as an artist. William Michael presently owns and operates six separate companies and affects over thirty plus households weekly. However successful he's been in business, William Michael believes in his principle that *the acceptance of failure is the beginning of success.* His belief is to, *"Live life as if it's your last day, do all you can do for others as long as it doesn't kill you, and to Leave more than you take."* This is the first fiction novel that he has written and is in the process of writing his first screenplay for his first movie project. Many of his influences came through the members of his family as in his parents and siblings, Otha Donald (late) & Josephine Priscilla Barbee; Jean Marie Barbee Wilson, Martia Yvonne

Barbee Jones, Donald Martin Barbee, and Mark Dayton Barbee.

In addition he acknowledges special influences in his life, but recognizes that their not limited to following: William Howard M. Griffith, Benjamin F. Jones, Elita Caldwell, Bishop Leonard R. Williams (late), Bishop Evelyn C. Williams/Gordon, Willie M. Williams (late), Bishop Claude Campbell, Elder Clarence Wright, Wade Trevor Rudolph, Richard A. Williams (late), Grover (late) & Flossie Cohen, Herbert L. Williams Sr. (late), Malachia & Katherine Brantley, Ronald Bryant Sr., Cong. Donald M. Payne, Gertrude Armour/Hicks, Troy Michael Williams, Bishops Joseph & Minerva Bell, Steven Barbee, Alan & Anita Sorrell, Roman (late) & Ella Hinnant, Joe & Louise Glover, James J. Williams, Walter McNeil, Joyce Brantley House, Elder Rosa Green (late), Lacy Brunson, Tommy Robinson, Elder Lawrence (late) & Sarah Powell, Alice J. Williams, Mary Nickelson, David & Gracie (late) Brantley, and Dr. Donald Womack (late). Other influences came through his extended Williams/Barbee and Zion Holy Church Families. He wishes to thank all that have blessed him throughout his life.

The Caretaker of Me

"Momma is everything to me. She's my hero, love and friend. She's the hope in my dreams, bravery in my spirit and the meaning to my being. It is she who enables me to be here today just to give you insights into my life. Whenever I think of my mom, she best reminds me of a mixture of Sisters Betty Shabazz and Maya Angelou; they both share in a strong physical resemblance. From the broadness of her hips and the flaring of her nostrils, momma along with Sisters Betty and Maya breathe life into those of us who they come in contact with. Her appearance is stereotypical of what a strong black mother would represent. Momma's stout in stature with draping shoulders, childbearing hips, skinny free and most of all, her face is painted by the wrinkles that are expressionistic of her life stories.

Spiritually, she possesses a sound silence that only tragedy and triumph teaches. Often without question, she has become a counselor to all hoping to seek guidance through a tunnel called religion. She'll

quietly lead you from the tunnel called
religion into your own awareness. Claiming
none, but accepting all, she'd unselfishly
share in her convictions. Her patience is
long and enduring, usually for the children
that she carried during their journeys into
infancy. Compromising her own body for
the safety of her children, she has welcomed
me into a safe haven called life. She is my
woman, strong, black, full-figured and
haughty, who is not ashamed to be woman.
Her femininity has taught me most of what it
means to be a man. I owe all that I have and
am to her. She owns this body, mind and
spirit. However beautiful, bold or strong,
she is the Caretaker of Me."

"I love you Mommy!"

Michael